DOCTORS &

BY THE SAME AUTHOR

Sweet Desserts
Varying Degrees of Hopelessness
Man or Mango? A Lament
Dot in the Universe

DOCTORS & NURSES

LUCY ELLMANN

BLOOMSBURY

The Origin of the World by Gustave Courbet (1866), Musée d'Orsay, Paris p. 29. Untitled work by Emily Gasquoine (2005), p. 119. Photograph of Stac Lee, St Kilda, Scotland by Stuart Murray/Scottish Natural Heritage/Centre for Ecology and Hydrology (2004), p. 205.

Published by Bloomsbury Publishing, New York and London
Distributed to the trade by Holtzbrinck Publishers

All papers used by Bloomsbury Publishing are natural, recyclable products made from wood grown in well-managed forests. The manufacturing processes conform to the environmental regulations of the country of origin.

Library of Congress Cataloging-in-Publication Data has been applied for.

ISBN-10: 1-59691-102-6
ISBN-13: 978-1-59691-102-4

First U.S. Edition 2006

1 3 5 7 9 10 8 6 4 2

Typeset by Hewer Text UK Ltd, Edinburgh
Printed by Quebecor World, Fairfield

ACKNOWLEDGEMENTS

I refute, abhor, deplore and CONDEMN acknowledgements in novels, as a craven attempt to implicate others in the author's crimes.

Otherwise, I would want to proclaim my gratitude to my editor, Alexandra Pringle, who has seen me through many torments, most of them self-induced. She's better than any grant, bursary, idol, patron, idle patron, or Arse Council endowment. The gal is GOOD.

(And anyway, she IS to blame for my writing novels.)

L.E.

For Katty Byrnes

Nothing: no thing: the non-existent: zero number: a thing or person of no significance or value: a worthless thing: a low condition: a trifle: (in Shakespeare) the vagina.

In the beginning there was no east or west, no above or below. There was no HORIZON. In the beginning there was all the fun of the fair! A jousting and a jostling, a rollering and a coastering, BIG BANGS, carbon dating, galaxies of cotton candy, and tasty morsels served on tectonic plates. Glaciers inglaciated themselves. There was fission, there was fusion. Everything was in FLUX. And for once, male and female came together as one.

It was deep, it was ROUGH, this mating, the violence of cliff against cataract, of mantle on magma. Lava spat far and wide as the ramming went on – the earth laid bare, fucked by a rock. The NOISE he made as he wedged himself into her, piercing her fissures, mashing a groove there that would last to the end of time. Juices sprang from the gully he dug and ran hot and sulphurous from her cracks. All the friction and fiction of lovemaking: he, brutish, relentless, refusing to be expelled; and she, passive, pinioned, helpless – except to envelop him further. His gnarled edges ploughed her moistened ground until she GROANED, the earth groaned and opened for a rock.

It might have gone on for ever, rock and gorge alone in the dark together on the brink of time. Why should he stop? Why should a rock ever stop snaking into the earth, why not rock her to and fro FOR EVER, rest, revive and TWIST there, never leave her be, shaft her for ETERNITY! But they were sadly interrupted: a sun was born, and its shrill white light shrivelled the wild will of the rock. Taking fright, he leapt backwards, landing upside-down in the sea about twenty miles away, a quarter-mile from shore, only his blunt tip showing above the waves. Gannets quickly nested there, on a foreskin of grass and guano. Their bodies made the ROCK look white, as if covered in his own cum.

The gorge was left to gape and gulp emptily at the air. Gradually she filled with water, the salt water of her own tears at first. But later she lost her tang and bubbled with now long-gone lacustrine creatures. A dinosaur named NIGEL once sipped from the forlorn swamp. People named LUCY bashed each other's skulls in on her banks, or ate the daffodils that grew there, hallucinated, and died.

Volcanic and erupting, as all cunts are, the lake sometimes heated up, red and swollen with desire, doubt, despair (curse of the unrequited), forcing her fish to die and her birds to fly. They flew to the ROCK, their arrival a clear message of love. The gannets fought them fiercely but the rock was unmoved, IMMOVABLE. His need: to hide from the sun in swirling waters, content with the indiscriminate fellatio he got from the rhythmic movements of the tide in the wide old ocean's gob.

It was the earliest, and earthiest, of betrayals.

A RURAL BACKWATER

A RURAL BACKWATER. Can't you see how FRIGHTENING that sounds? Sounds like a place in which you might quietly DROWN. Birds tweeting overhead, late-afternoon sun flickering across the water, moorhens, greenery, dandelion FAIRIES floating by . . . A quick skinny-dip before anyone notices! But as soon as you get in, mud sucks at your feet and strong slimy weeds tug at your arms. The temperature of the water takes your breath away and you start to SINK. Before you know it, your eyes, still open, are being nibbled by STICKLEBACKS, your grey cheeks tickled by feathery fronds. Hey, somebody call an AMBULANCE, for chrissake!

There is no possibility of avoiding a walk today – no taxis at the station. As soon as she reaches the pavement, Jen is almost RUN OVER: a big truck starts to move off just as she tries to squeeze past it. Jen could easily have been CAUGHT by that truck, pulled along by some bit of her clothing or, more probably, her HANDBAG, which she wears diagonally across her chest to deter BAG-SNATCHERS. Jen could have been snatched herself by that truck and pulled slowly along the road, so slowly at first she might have been able to keep up with it for a bit by running backwards beside the truck, much to the amusement of passers-by, much to the amusement of her ENEMIES, who would glory in Jen's befuddlement followed by her EXTINCTION beneath the many wheels of the many-wheeled truck after her ridiculous attempt to stay alive by running backwards no doubt yelling 'HELP!' or 'STOP!' or 'WAIT!' or some other unmemorable last word. But Jen's enemies will have to wait a little longer for the pleasure of seeing her SQUISHED FLAT.

Jen's hot and her foot hurts. Her feet always hurt. Amazing that feet work AT ALL. Guy standing on the corner, talking into his mobile phone. Looks like he's lecturing the street! Looks like an IDIOT. She smells something. A tree. Where's the nice stinky tree? She retraces a few steps to try to smell it again. The trouble is, Jen runs out of smelling ABILITY very quickly. She gets a HEADACHE if she sniffs too long.

Hot. Need a HAIRCUT. Need to put my hair up. Boxes. Need boxes. Hot. Pink. Sweaty. Sore foot. Hair. Job interview. VOMIT: pink-noodle vomit on the street! Who'd eat that? Dog maybe. Pink POODLE perhaps. Better than Urma Thurb's food though. Her and her soft-boiled eggs and her fucking blueberry YOGHURTS, sitting there like KATHARINE HEPBURN in that office of hers like she's the QUEEN OF SHEBA. Urma Thurb used to be NICE, used to LISTEN when you talk to her. Now she's too busy. HATES everyone. New man, new job, FUCK YOU.

Guy eating breakfast in his front room, reading the paper. Enormous paper, tiny egg. They should print the news ON the egg. Turn the chair into a commode so he could have his morning CRAP there too. Jen has read the paper today (she collected all the newspapers on the train that other people left behind), including an obituary of the woman who discovered the first COELACANTH; there was a picture of her KISSING the coelacanth she had identified, after it was stuffed. Yiiigghhh. And now the coelacanth woman herself is dead. Who *knows* what death takes out of you, how long the moment of DISSOLUTION might be, or how terrible? This worried CHARLOTTE BRONTË a lot.

Teenager blocking the path. Jen longs to elbow her in the ribs. Jen has VIOLENT IMAGES of how IN LOVE everyone is, violent because of what she wants to DO to them. Every buoyant babe on the street, every eyebrowless damsel in the magazines – all seem to BEG to have their little lives curtailed.

Bunch of dopes at the bus-stop, secretly wanking: they have that bored look of people when they're secretly wanking. Jen wants a CHEESE SANDWICH. Hates EVERYONE. Or maybe tuna fish. Dog barking. Pink poodle? Rape victim in the paper. Rape VICTIM, the woman insisted, not rape SURVIVOR. Jen has been raped enough to know that all men hate her, the last time DRUGGED, so that she woke to find scratches on her inner thighs and had to GUESS the rest. Nobody BELIEVED her. Too FAT to be believed, too fat to be LISTENED to. Now she sees rape-eyed women everywhere. They walk the earth unpitied. All anyone really wants is to be left in charge of their own GENITALS.

Jen's hatreds are immodest – they are not confined to herself alone! She loathes widely. Hates her species and her nation too, its gardens and gonads and government, the fox-hunts and football and FAILURE, the ETHOS of failure. Nigella Lawson, Neighbourhood Watch Schemes, the BUSH – they talk about Africa as if they still OWN it!

She hates the BBC, the NHS, Bhs, HSB, the DHSS, B & Q, R & B, B & Bs, the BMJ, BMs, BMXs, C & A, M & S, H & M, HMV, TCP, TLC, CCTV, CPR, ECGs, ENT, the C of E, the EU, the QE2, DIY, MFI, MRIs, SRNs, ICUs, IVF, IDS, IDs, PMT, BUPA, UFOs, VIPs, JCBs, GCSEs, CVs, STDs, MPs, PMs, GPs, WPCs, WCs, QCs, OBEs, OAPs, the SAS, MI5, MI6, MI7, MI8, MI9, etc, the KGB, KLM, AK-47s, HGVs, GBH, G8, ITV, DNA, the FA, the PO, P & O, G & Ts, RSVPs, BYOBs, the CIA, the IRA, the UK, the USA, LA, CO_2, H_2O, and OJ. (But she LIKES BLTs!)

She hates everyone she's ever met! She hates her whole FAMILY (though her brother's all that's left). She hates their neighbours in the building, because THEY get to carry on living there and she DOESN'T (the family flat where she has spent her ENTIRE LIFE, now up for sale against her wishes). Must be glad to see the back of me. They like my back view BEST, like to see me DEPARTING. That's how I like THEM too. Like to see people moving rapidly AWAY from me. Only way to stop them STARING all the time.

Jen feels she's being stared at NOW, as she peers across the street at what appears to be a café. So hungry! Hot. Hungry. Hair. Job interview. You need to EAT something before a JOB INTERVIEW. But Jen's torn between wanting to get to the café and wanting to deprive potential STARERS of something to stare at. Sometimes they lose interest if you FREEZE. But you can't freeze in the middle of the ROAD, with CARS coming.

THE CAFÉ

Jen sits for TWENTY MINUTES in her booth without being SERVED. The waitress consistently ignores her. Jen has changed her mind about the sandwich: now she wants CAKE. She's read the menu, verified they HAVE cake. Why, she's seen it with her own eyes! But no waitress. The place is full of babies. No COMPETING with all these babies. Who gave mothers permission to take over cafés? What do BABIES know about CAKE?

One kid keeps creeping over and THROWING things at her. No ELBOW ROOM in this booth – feels like a COFFIN. I'm going to DIE in here, waiting for cake. Where is the fucking serving wench? Hiding behind the counter probably, devouring all the cake. Then she pukes it back on to the plate. People are always hiring these skinny waitresses on the assumption that they're ABSTEMIOUS. But what if they're BULIMIC and will cost you a fortune in doughnuts?

She somehow senses that I don't DESERVE cake. But HOW, without even LOOKING at me, how does she know I'm unworthy of cake? Somebody come round earlier and WARN everybody? Like those guys who used to have to walk ahead of the train, waving a little flag. 'Cake-eater on her way – don't GIVE her any!'

By the time the waitress finally happens upon her in her

booth, Jen is CRYING. What does the waitress think that IS on Jen's face? SWEAT? That's blood, sweat and tears, honey! And now she's set all the OTHER babies off!

'Could I have a piece of your pear, apple and bramble cake, please?' innocently asks Jen. The waitress denies they *have* any such cake. WHY MUST PEOPLE DO THIS? When the cake in its ENTIRETY is sitting right behind her – Jen's been STARING at it for half an hour!

WHAT A DUMP. Doesn't she know we're all only a week from STARVATION? You need to be in constant reach of food, water, shelter, light, TV, newspapers, alcohol, umbrellas, escalators, cigarettes and movies: it's our HABITAT. Venture far from this stuff and you're taking a BIG RISK (and missing movies). You're better off being held hostage by Colombian GUERRILLAS than stumbling through the jungle on your own. At least with the guerrillas you'll get food and a bed, maybe even a drink and a date! Being alone is only really safe if you're a TREE.

Trees have it made. Plonk themselves down on a reliable food source and sit tight for CENTURIES, their leaves swept away by the wind and rain, their seeds transported by birds. WE have to keep on the move. Otherwise we'd be surrounded by SHIT. This is why the first creatures started CREEPING: they had to get away from their shit and their CHILDREN.

We only *go* to cafés because we assume there will be FOOD there, and a place to shit. Cafés with no toilet soon go out of business –

The waitress suddenly reappears, MIT CAKE. But it's TINY. What is this miserable minuscule MINNIE MOUSE piece of cake? Jen has waited too long. One lousy PRISSY piece of cake just ain't gonna do it. She wants the WHOLE CAKE, in its ENTIRETY, in fact she wants to eat the whole PLACE, mothers, babies, urchins and all! She wants to eat the bloody SERVING WENCH too, KING KONG-style, clutching that slender waist in her big fat fist while she bites her stupid HEAD off, cups, saucers, forks, knives, chairs, tables, doors and windows whizzing out of the corner of Jen's mouth as CAKE CAKE CAKE pours down her GULLET into her GIZZARD (or vice versa), apples, pears and brambles, not an air pocket to be found in there between the CAKE and the SERVING WENCH and the weird metallic taste of the pretentious antique CASH REGISTER.

Instead, Jen merely asks if she can buy the rest of the cake 'to take home'. No. Why not? Because then there would be no pear, apple and bramble cake to offer OTHER customers, should they arrive EXPECTING to find a pear, apple and bramble cake. But why does it MATTER who buys the cake, so long as it's sold to SOMEBODY? There are plenty of OTHER cakes for those dopes. What the hell does it matter if this particular cake is sold to ONE dope or a BUNCH of dopes? JEN WANTS CAKE.

She wants anything she WANTS today. She has just arrived in a RURAL BACKWATER. She has almost been RUN OVER, she has been stared at, jeered at, denied cake. She has already had a little CRY. Jen is all alone in a strange place, motherless, fatherless, friendless and blue, blue as the sky outside, SKY-BLUE – a colour Jen has hated since infancy, when her mother forced her to take naps in her sky-blue bedroom. CAKE is her simple request! But nobody listens.

Jen gets up, releasing a stinging fart, and heads for the loo. BUT THERE IS NO LOO. Call this a CAFÉ?

THE CORRIDOR

She stared down the corridor. It was not a LONG corridor, nor a very wide one. It was not a corridor worth mentioning THREE TIMES, but still it got mentioned.

Jen was a bit surprised to find herself standing in the bleak and narrow corridor (FOUR) of a rural GP's surgery, waiting to be interviewed for the nurse's job. She was not unaware that MOST doctor–nurse books start with the job-interview scene. No, that was not what surprised her. What surprised her was that SHE was a nurse.

Though she panted all the time, and stank, she was a nurse. Though she was so fat she attracted notice going through doorways, in case she didn't MAKE it, she was a nurse. Though a light snow of DANDRUFF drifted down whenever she twiddled with her hair, which she did quite often, she was a nurse. Though every hair on her head was split, frizzed and frazzled, her neck a cascade of chins, she was a nurse. Though, squidlike, she changed COLOUR all the time, still she was a nurse (sometimes a pink one, sometimes black-and-blue). Though she'd barely passed all her EXAMS and was off sick half the time she was meant to be on duty, she was a nurse. Though she would rather NOT cure anybody if she could help it, she was a nurse. Though she'd been taught to see patients as DISEASES, and diseases as STATISTICS, she was a nurse. Though she had a deep aversion to the SICK, the

AGED, and the DISABLED, she was a nurse. OK, so she hated oldies, cripples and retards. Everyone has their LIMIT. (They hated HER too!) She didn't much like KIDS either.

Shifting roomily in her trademark cargo pants, Jen tried to remember why she'd come. One reason was that nursing EXISTS, as a job. If it didn't, she wouldn't have bothered applying for a nursing position. Hell, she wouldn't have done all that TRAINING either. The other reason is that JEN exists. If she didn't, she wouldn't have NEEDED a job, she could have hovered ethereally somewhere: just being a couple of interrelated ATOMS would do.

Jen had often considered NOT existing. She was conversant with all the latest fashions in self-immolation. She could have clamped her head in a vice and bored holes in her temple with an electric drill, or set about her throat with an electric carving-knife. She could have injected herself with a little MAYONNAISE or PEANUT BUTTER, or tried a combo of potassium chloride, sodium thiopental and pancuronium bromide (the recipe on Death Row), or raided the hospital labs for a smidgin of SMALLPOX. She could have drunk raw hydrochloric acid with a chaser of LIT FIRECRACKERS (always a big hit in the hospital canteen). But in the end it seemed simpler to get a job. Nursing was in her BLOOD (Jen was rather careless with needles) and – DUTY IS ALL.

Her most recent job had been on the Children's Ward of a big city hospital: shit everywhere, pisspots overflowing. Children froze to death in the hallways awaiting a bed. The place looked like it hadn't been cleaned since Victorian times (the cleaners were on some kind of CONTRACT). It was MURDER, it was MAYHEM, it was the NHS during a period of reform, and Jen had called it home for a time.

Although many children died under her care (more than the national AVERAGE, if anyone had bothered to check), Jen was considered a useful member of staff. She could always be relied on to sit by a dying kid's bed all night and still have the energy to make QUIPS in the morning with the grieving parents about the kid's final thrashings or the effect of projectile vomiting on her UNIFORM. And she it was who volunteered to accompany seriously ill children in the ambulance to specialist (BETTER) hospitals which, curiously, they never reached in time.

Jen had also proved invaluable to the ward sister, Urma Thurb, to whom she brought secret nips of WHISKY, and *Take a Break* magazine hot off the press. They ate lunch together, Urma Thurb pecking at a blueberry yoghurt while Jen chomped through some of the many cheese sandwiches she kept in her voluminous handbag. Jen had formed a rather profound ATTACHMENT to Urma Thurb, in fact. HAPPY DAYS, until Urma Thurb went and married TONY, the hospital ODD-JOB MAN, and started spending more and more time at home, making CUSTARD by CANDLELIGHT, or whatever it is wifelets DO.

Jen was left high and dry! She was always getting involved this way with women she admired and subsequently HATED. Abandoned by Urma Thurb, Jen wandered through the X-ray department during her spare time, hoping to soak up some leaked radiation, or sat alone in the salmonella-rife canteen, slouched over egg dishes. She charted and chased the spread of MRSA infections through the hospital, in an effort to CATCH one and get a bit of SYMPATHY and a few days off. She failed. Her only triumph was when she managed to persuade a gullible surgeon to take out her perfectly healthy APPENDIX, a painful ordeal that Jen appreciated in complex ways. She played with the wound afterwards, inserting various dirty objects and substances to make it worse. But it healed.

When Urma Thurb switched officially to part-time work, Jen resorted to hanging around the sperm-donor unit, sucking the cocks of junior doctors to help them augment their tiny incomes. (They, and Urma Thurb, were responsible for the somewhat ambivalent REFERENCES that now lurked, damp but intact, in a commodious compartment of her cargo pants.)

Oh, Jen had once been the life and soul of the PARTY! During all-night sessions in the nurses' digs in her student days, Jen had taken on a quarter or fifth of those present, in her mouth, her cunt, or her ass. She'd been rammed up against the back of a motorway CAR-WASH once, by three or four smiling lorry drivers she never saw again. She'd been fucked by a whole QUEUE of guys in the park! She had even entered upon a tricky, sort of ICKY, affair with an ageing OSTEOPATH who'd daily screwed her senseless, beaten her with an ornate Tibetan hammer, and told her when to go to the LOO. She'd plunged her whole face into many a fleshy VULVA too.

AEROPLANES

A door was suddenly flung open halfway down the corridor (five). A woman came rushing out in tears and nearly crashed into JEN. Another candidate for the nurse's job? What had they DONE to her in there? Jen was about to turn on her heels, her sore HEELS, and quietly retreat, back to the WOMB if necessary. But a man was already bellowing, 'NEXT!' Always there is duty.

Conscious of her blunt and bloated form, the dark thicket of hair obscuring the CLIFF FACE of her forehead, her tiny mouth, unintentionally smug, puckered between ballooning cheeks, Jen advanced down the corridor (seven) to the open doorway. But there was no firing squad in there after all, just a guy up a ladder, painting the ceiling! Must be the wrong room. Jen was about to waddle back out into the corridor (eight), when the man on the ladder said, without looking at Jen, 'Never mind *her*, silly woman. All I said was that she should lose some weight! Obesity is the biggest strain on NHS resources. Have a seat. Hope you don't mind if I just finish this before the paint dries. Everything looks better with a nice new coat of white paint, don't you think? Now, what seems to be the problem?'

So he was the DOCTOR. And he seemed to think Jen was a PATIENT! Eager to correct this mistake (who wants to be a patient?), Jen stumbled towards what looked like a chair, hidden under a dustsheet. Her stumble was nothing to do with OBESITY or varicose veins or sciatica or lumbago or rickets or torn ligaments or even OSGOOD-SCHLATTER disease. Jen stumbled because she had *recognised* the man on the ladder! He was the HERO OF THE HOUR on a plane trip she'd taken a few years before!

AEROPLANES HAVE RUINED THE WORLD. They are the source of all human misery. Not just because of their primarily MILITARY purpose, nor the pollution and the solid blocks of frozen SHIT they rain down on us, nor how horrifically they crash, when they do. Nor is it the lethal trolleys full of lethal FOOD that catapult over everybody during thunderstorms. Nor the reclining seats, that recline your stupid head right into the lap of the jerk sitting behind you. Nor is it because of the CHEESY SNAX they give you whether you like cheese or *not*. Nor the TB you catch from the so-called VENTILATION system, nor the VD you get from the Mile High Club, nor the DVT that gets YOU if you forget to put on your deep-vein-thrombosis SOCKS.

No. The worst thing about aeroplanes is that, BECAUSE of them, you are expected to attend every goddamn wedding, funeral, baby shower, circumcision and retirement do on the PLANET, depending on where your friends and relatives have decided to live, die, quit or get married. BECAUSE OF AEROPLANES you have to drag your sorry ass to every dumb party these people put on! Or they come to YOU. If you're really unlucky, the American PRESIDENT flies in clutching a plastic turkey on a tray. Aeroplanes show no mercy.

It is OBSCENE, is it not, to be sucked across an entire CONTINENT without seeing a single flower or a bird (FUCK Lake Tahoe FUCK the Alps), just so that you can GET somewhere and VISIT somebody and eat and eat until you EXPLODE, the shit backed up in there for MILES because you never feel at ease in your relative's BATHROOM.

Jen was on her way home from the HIGH-SCHOOL GRADUATION of some DISTANT COUSIN in California. There she was, sprawled across three seats, minding her own business, watching a Bruce Willis movie and wearing her deep-vein-thrombosis socks, when a stewardess ran shrieking down the aisle, warning people that there was a woman at the front of the plane who had a GUN and was threatening to shoot all the CHILDREN.

Great. So, along with the radiation exposure and economy-class AIR and Bruce Willis (you can't hear a THING that guy SAYS on a plane, he mumbles so), Jen was now expected to allow herself to be MURDERED. And all because her distant cousin hadn't managed to screw up high school.

Jen grabbed the first kid that came along, to use as a HUMAN SHIELD. If the gun-woman came her way, she was hoping to DISTRACT her with the KID, thereby gaining crucial time for her own cumbrous getaway. Jen held on to that kid for an HOUR (his mother had no idea what had HAPPENED to him!) but there was still no sign of the gun-woman, no slaughtering of innocents, no loss of CABIN PRESSURE. Not even any cheesy snax! Like all emergency situations, there were longueurs.

Jen finally abandoned her kid shield (now either asleep or *unconscious* from being squeezed so hard) and wandered up to the front to see what was going on. A crowd had gathered in the galley amongst all the lethal trolleys and secret stashes of barbiturates for the stewardesses. At the centre of it was a DOCTOR who, it seemed, had SINGLE-HANDEDLY wrestled the gun-toting woman to the floor, snatched her weapon (a fake revolver she'd got in Disneyland), tied her up, sedated her, and even listened to her HARD-LUCK STORY until she conked out. He was the HERO OF THE HOUR: he had risked his life to save the plane!!!

Intrigued, Jen pressed through the throng, pushing a few people OVER to get a glimpse of the daring doc. He had blond hair and grey eyes and a cleft chin and trim waist and hips! He was also nicely SILHOUETTED against a porthole, as he patiently answered a lot of damn fool questions (these were not MEDICAL people) about the woman and her motives and her MOTHER (she apparently thought she'd SPOTTED her mother outside the plane somewhere over Greenland, and had wanted to shoot all the children to PROTECT them from her mother). The doctor was sharing several theories he'd just formulated about the woman, mothers, Disneyland (HE'D been there too!), the effects of high altitudes on the human psyche, and other two-bit notions until everybody was SICK of the woman and her fucking childhood, even a bit sick of the DOCTOR. Civilians are so FICKLE.

As people began to drift back to their seats and Bruce Willis, Jen was able to get closer to the doctor, JEN, who was suffering GUT ACHE, so keen was she to get the Hero of the Hour into one of the aeroplane LOOS. She had always been susceptible to GLORY and, in particular, doctors in EMERGENCY SITUATIONS. Sure enough, the obliging doc was soon in the loo, clutching at Jen's enormous ass with the compulsive gestures of a hero in the throes of passion in very cramped conditions. It was all over in a JIFFY, too soon to catch a disease or each other's name.

THE JOB INTERVIEW

Jen didn't see the dishy doc again during the flight, so she hadn't incurred the usual REBUFF (few were not immediately ashamed of having fucked her), and was therefore able to consider the encounter a TRIUMPH, requiring frequent RE-ENACTMENTS (no KNOWING how much masturbation it takes to keep a vessel like Jen afloat). And now here he was in a RURAL BACKWATER, held aloft on a cloud of whiteness – his white coat, his white paint – as he restored his ceiling to its original and much-deserved PALLOR. He, all unknowing and immersed in his paint job, did not even glance at Jen. SHE, plopping into a chair, had no interest in being HIRED any more, only DESIRED.

'So – what seems to be the problem?' he asked again.

The art of flirtation has taken many a knock. There wasn't much left of it in Jen besides sweat, the odd LEER, and small-talk bordering on the INSANE. But she did her best.

'Well, you see, doctor, it's my ASS.'

He turned, astounded, took in her gargantuan form and, whether from chagrin at his previous speech on obesity, or just dread of having to examine THAT ASS, he swayed, hollered, lost his balance and fell – into Jen's LAP, along with his pot of white paint. From there he slid awkwardly to the floor. The paint swirling between her legs looked like CREAM: Jen was tempted to lick it up, but duty called.

She reached down to wrench the squirming doctor back into an upright position.

'Are you all right?' she asked as she yanked.

'Are YOU?' he quirked. Doctors quirk a LOT. Nobody knows exactly what quirking IS, or why they do it; it's just a medical fact.

Jen began dabbing at his hair with a dustsheet. He was about to do the same to JEN when Francine, the evil receptionist (every GP *has* one), came in carrying a tray of tea and biscuits. Good medical practice revolves around plenty of hot drinks, accompanied by BICKIES and CHOCKIES (donated by duped, grateful or bamboozled patients), and CIGGIES. When not providing such delicacies, Francine busied herself dissuading people from making APPOINTMENTS – unless they were actually DYING (in which case they were unlikely to attend). She was FAMOUS for the sheer number of weeping mothers she'd managed to turn away, along with their feverish infants. Now she made herself useful by formally introducing Jen to the doctor.

He recovered as best he could from his fall and the revelation that Jen was not another boring PATIENT (she looked sick enough!) but instead the only candidate for the nursing job. *Jen* was dismayed by something else. She didn't like his NAME: Roger Lewis. A name full of anticlimax, full of COLLAPSE, the sexual explicitness of the ROGER so quickly refuted by the loose, limp LEWIS, which sounds like 'less'. UNHAPPY NAME, an injunction to FUCK LESS!

Anita LOOS is a name with some VITALITY. Roger Lewis sounds like something WINDING DOWN, dwindling to nothing! Like goldfish shit, it TRAILS disappointingly: Lewisssssss. A name that contains its own HECKLE, its own hiss. A name empty of promise, hope or joy! No good can come of a name like ROGER LEWIS. No PHILANTHROPIST ever came with a name like that, no CASANOVA. (Also, Jen had a little problem with her R's, which meant that, without supreme EFFORT on her part, there would be two W's in his name whenever she pronounced it, which is far too many. Woger Lewis: wimpy, weasly, woebegone words!)

Paint had by now curdled in every crevice of her cargo pants. But Jen was used to feeling sodden, and at least this time she would leave a puddle of PAINT in her chair when she got up, not SWEAT. It even occurred to her that Dr Lewis might feel he HAD to give her the job now, out of shame at having soaked her! The thought was cheering. But she was still disconcerted by his failure to RECOGNISE her. Perhaps he never would!?

His aloofness chilled her, but the tea warmed her. Then the coffee. Then more TEA. And still the hot drinks kept coming, along with the doctor's probing QUESTIONS, as he delineated one onerous nursy task after another in excruciating detail. What's a girl to DO when a fellow drones on so? A SNORE erupted from Jen, which drew the interview at last to a close.

Rising from his swivel seat, Dr Lewis gave Jen a poke on the shoulder and asked, 'How would you like to see the flat that comes with the job?'

A little annoyed at first at being woken from such a pleasant snooze, Jen followed Dr Lewis out into the corridor (eleven) and waited while he unlocked a door and trotted down some steep steps to switch the lights on. Jen was not all that keen on the idea of living ON THE PREMISES. She'd assumed she'd have to rent some revolting BEDSIT with FARM CHILDREN picking their noses outside her window all day, but at least she'd have privacy in which to EAT amply, away from the stern gaze of COLLEAGUES. She didn't want Woger and Fwancine to hear her evewy FART late into the night! (Also, living on the premises is always an invitation to your employer to work you like a DOG.)

When he called her, she tremulously tiptoed down the stairs. She expected to find a fully equipped TORTURE

CHAMBER down there. Who wants to live in a BASEMENT? Jen was prepared for ropes, chains, a hanging CAGE, she was prepared to be MURDERED. But it turned out to be a small, plain, one-bedroom flat, the kind of place in which an abstemious single woman might eat a soft-boiled egg and consider herself LUCKY, the radio on softly in the background and her underpants drying over a sink full of TEA LEAVES.

Dr Lewis led Jen into the gloomy bathroom where he proudly pointed out the jacuzzi. 'One of the perks of the job,' he quirked. 'Besides working with *me*, that is!'

Jen WAS impressed with the jacuzzi – unlike most baths it looked big enough to accommodate her! She looked up at Dr Lewis hungrily (she'd only had about a dozen biscuits) and asked, 'Does this mean you're offering me the job?'

'No one else applied!' he burbled happily.

This wasn't entirely true. There had been a few other applicants but, after listening to Dr Lewis explain every damn thing over the phone for hours at a time, none of them had turned up for the interview! Anyway, he didn't WANT them. There was something about Jen, something ENORMOUS, something unfathomable. Staring across the jacuzzi at Jen's JACKSIE, Dr Lewis decided that one day he would indulge in vigorous sexual intercourse with this woman, making use of both the front bottom and the back!

For the ANIMAL in Dr Lewis wanted to PEE in exultation at having found a new nurse – he planned to work her like a DOG. The animal in JEN wanted to grab Dr Lewis by the scruff of the neck, haul him off to a corner of her den and EAT him.

There was a good deal of common ground between them.

JEN'S BODY

Embryos are all HYALINE CARTILAGE, and Jen was no exception. Within a month of her conception she was a quarter of an inch long and her heart was beating. A month later, she had eyes but no eyelids. A week later she had inner ears.

How can you just HATE all this? But she does.

By the time she was born Jen had three hundred and fifteen bones. When she reached full skeletal maturity at the age of twenty, she had two hundred and six! (She didn't LOSE any, they just joined together a bit over the years.) Only about half of the twenty-nine bones in Jen's head are in her FACE. Her skull is a little dented from a tumble she took on a train as a baby.

She's got trapezoid, trapezium, scaphoid, lunate, pisiform, triquetral, capitate, hamate, metacarpal and phalanx bones in her hands, one finger slightly shorter than it should be (she got it caught in a car door at the age of eleven). Her sacrum's connected to her ilium's connected to her pubis's connected to her acetabulum's connected to the balls of her femurs, the longest bones in Jen's body. Jen's got an ISCHIUM in her ASS! Then there's her patella and her tibia and her fibula and her FEET (her sore feet!), which have all the usual astragalus, metatarsal, calcaneum, navicular, cuneiform, cuboid, trochlea and phalanx bones.

Padding the junctions, as Jen pads about, is more CARTILAGE. There's not much room in Jen's hands for MUSCLES, so ligaments pull her fingers around. Ligaments also hold her WOMB in place, her breasts (somewhat), and the lenses of her EYES. She's got sinews and tendons too. She's got it all! There's a tendon in Jen's heart that makes it PUMP. Selfish heart! It pumps blood to ITSELF first.

You could divide Jen up in various ways. Her body is maintained by a number of interrelated SYSTEMS: digestive, excretory, respiratory, reproductive, skeletal, integument (skin), muscular, endocrine, cardiovascular, and lymph-vascular. Also TISSUES, plenty of tissues. And MEMBRANES: synovial membranes and serous membranes and mucous membranes and villi and meninges and PERIOSTEUM.

There are a lot of PROCESSES going on in her too: circulation and ovulation and acidosis and agglutination and dyscrasia and desquamation and catabolism and anabolism and homeostasis and haemolysis and miosis and osmosis and oxidation and filtration and dilation and salivation and depolarisation and ossification and supination and ptosis and proprioception and GOOSEBUMPS and perspiration and pigmentation and presbyacusis and a permanently runny nose and electrical stuff going on in her head and coagulation and KIDNEYS.

Jen's kidneys are full of tiny TUBES, so many tubes! Each of her kidneys has thousands of NEPHRONS, that contain a knot of CAPILLARIES called a GLOMERULUS, which sits inside a BOWMAN'S CAPSULE, shaped something like a HUNTING HAT (but without the feather). Jen's blood is filtered through these capillaries at A LITRE A MINUTE, twelve hundred litres a DAY. She is tenacious of life!

Jen's liver weighs four pounds and produces BARREL-

LOADS of bile, stored by the BUSHEL in Jen's gall bladder. Her bile is released into her small intestine through her Sphincter of Oddi. Enzymes and alkaline juices come out of her Crypts of Lieberkühn to neutralise her stomach acid. Her Islets of Langerhans produce insulin. She's got six salivary glands and between them they squirt out about THIRTY PINTS of saliva a WEEK (MORE if she sees cake).

Jen's oesophagus is ten inches long; her duodenum too. Jen's jejunum's EIGHT FEET, her ilium's twelve. Her colon's about four and a half. There are ACRES of gut in Jen, thirty-five feet of it to be precise, held in place by mesenteries, like PUPPET STRINGS, attached to her peritoneum. (Her appendix is no more.)

Jen's blood SPIRALS through her veins and arteries: it's the best way to travel! Her heart and lungs are separated from her digestive organs by her diaphragm. Jen breathes rapidly, about twenty-five times a MINUTE (but still she feels out of breath!). The smallest cells in her body are PLATELETS. She's got a million of 'em! They live about four days. Her red blood cells are DOUGHNUT-shaped, and live for four months. Her white cells live SIX months and can CREEP (her pus is full of DEAD ones that don't creep any more). Her muscle and nerve cells are long and thin, her liver cells HEXAGONAL.

Jen's brain is 85% water. The left and right sides of it are bridged by a CORPUS CALLOSUM – otherwise Jen might STRANGLE herself by accident! Her putamen, part of the basal ganglia in the middle of her brain, makes it possible for Jen to ride a bike without THINKING about it (if she WANTED to ride a bike, which she DOESN'T). Her hypothalamus tells her autonomic nervous system what to do, which is quite helpful. Jen has eighty-six major nerves, along with all that tenuous, frightening stuff like motor neurones and Schwann cells and dendrites and glia and myelin sheaths, and a few nodes of Ranvier.

Jen has olfactory BULBS, but no ADENOIDS, and she wants them back! (How dare doctors fool with your organs before you know what's what?) She also has nine thousand taste buds (and makes good use of them!). Her tongue is triangular, and apart from her trouble with R's, moves with extreme efficiency, thanks to her palatoglossus, styloglossus and hyoglossus muscles – you need a different muscle for everything! How BEAUTIFULLY Jen's muscles drape her body, if you could only SEE them. Her gluteus maximus is MAGNIFICENT. Also, her adductor magnus, her rectus femoris, her gastrocnemius (calf muscle) and her brachioradialis (forearm). The muscle in Jen's heart, her Bundle of His, is in fact *hers*.

Jen has no hair on her LIP skin, but she's got a hundred and twenty-eight thousand hairs on her head! She has hair shafts and hair FOLLICLES. Sweat glands and apocrine glands have been emitting sexual smells since she reached puberty. Her skin also has keratin and pain receptors and melanocytes that distribute pigment. She has Meissner's corpuscles (that detect touch), Pacinian corpuscles (pressure), Ruffini corpuscles (warmth), and Krauss corpuscles (cold). Sometimes Krauss and Ruffini battle it out all day! She's got STRETCH MARKS too, which do nobody any good. But because of her skin Jen is: WATERPROOF.

How can a person HATE all this? But she does.

Jen pisses five pints a day and shits up a STORM. Her shit is 75% water. It's taken away like everybody else's and subjected to the same shit-reduction MEASURES, but there's so much MORE of hers. She is using up more than her fair share of NATURAL RESOURCES. She requires so much! The EARTH weighs more because Jen is here.

When not in uniform, Jen wears CARGO PANTS, DUNGAREES really, which act as a kind of TENT for her WHOLE BODY. Never has an ass looked so big. But Jen's ass doesn't concern her (it's been NUMB for years!). What Jen secretly loves is her CUNT. She's got labia minora AND majora! Two bulbocavernous muscles, a fossa navicularis, a levator ani muscle, and a portio vaginalis uteri. Tags of skin called carunculae myrtiformes are all that's left of Jen's HYMEN. Her vagina's lined with squamous epithelium – it stinks like a SQUAM CREEK OYSTER!

Jen's cunt is a place of untold incident and unpredictable sensation. It has been left to lie fallow for long periods, it has ATROPHIED between bouts of abuse. It has itched, farted and drooled, it has failed to DELIVER. And yet – she LOVES it! She's charmed by its quiet steadfastness, how LEVEL it stays as she walks, her two feet stepping out ahead but her cunt following right along, like a third FOOT peeking out from under its hood of stomach flab.

In a better world, cunts would LEAD THE WAY. The PENIS, with all its ACROBATICS, has stolen the show while the CUNT, that anarchic, amorphous, seething, seeking, salty mound of anchored flesh, is left to fester, hidden and ignored. With it women's LUST and ANGER are hidden – until they stink to high heaven! The CUNT is the black hole of the universe that astronomers keep warning us about (BAD NEWS for the astronaut in his PRIAPIC HOOD): they have sullied the COSMOS with their CUNT-FEAR!

All Jen really wants to TALK about is her cunt. This is what MOST women want to talk about. There's a deep insincerity and sadness amongst women because they DON'T talk about their cunts (except to complain about thrush or menstruation, or to describe CHILDBIRTH in exquisite detail). The cunt is UNMENTIONABLE. It's been forced underground. Substitutes have had to be found. Women do their hair in HONOUR of their cunts. They parade new clothes in SERVICE to their cunts. They accentuate their eyes (dark and glistening and hairy), their mouths (pink and wet), in IMITATION of their cunts. The cunt is their PURPOSE.

And they were once so proud!

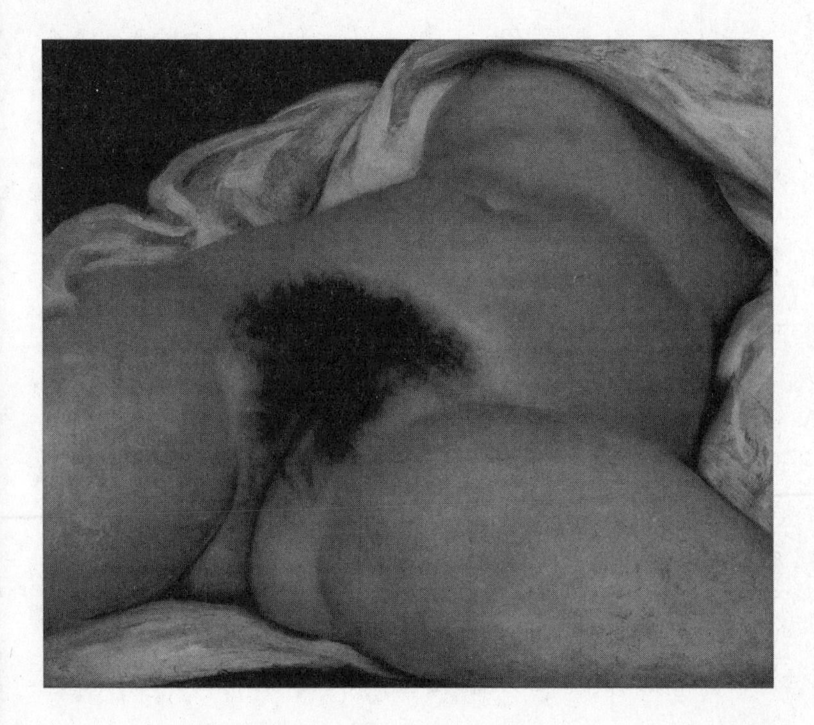

I HAVE A JOB!

Jen has been through all the diminishment of moving, of seeing her junk reduced to compact units measured by the cubic centimetre. It's like seeing your own COFFIN. Cardboard boxes attest your expendability, your flexibility, your lack of significance in the world: YOU ARE EPHEMERAL. The shame then, to see grown men struggling up the stairs with your piano!

JEN has no piano (she only ever played the CLARINET, and that not very well). What Jen has are BOXES, so many boxes! She alone knows what's IN them. They have been packed resentfully and with care. But there's no time to UNPACK them now. Jen has to go to WORK. It's her first day! Jen has a job. People say this – 'I HAVE A JOB' – as if nobody ELSE has a job. But almost every other dumb cluck in the WORLD has a job. BIG DEAL.

Emerging from her den at eight in the morning, Jen found only Francine in the surgery. Francine had just settled down to a nice steaming hot cup of tea, and was deflecting the few phone calls coming in while fucking with her nails (BITING them mostly). She was caked in all the accoutrements of BEAUTY: beauty products. She looked like a BEAUTICIAN, Jen's least favourite profession. BARBIE DOLLS: they think they OWN beauty. Francine's elaborate amount of make-up signalled at least a close ACQUAINTANCE with beauticians that Jen could never share.

Eyeing Francine therefore with apprehension, Jen asked, 'Where's Dr Lewis?'

'Upstairs,' Francine replied blandly.

'What's he doing up there?'

'He LIVES there – didn't you KNOW? Yeah, he lives in the attic.'

'With his, uh, WIFE?' asked Jen tensely.

'Oh, no. She left him a few years back. He got the kids, though.'

'Oh?'

'Yeah, Edward and Adele. But they shouldn't bother you much. They're not allowed in here.'

Kids? Jen had turned a little green. Francine was *watching* her change colour. To thwart her, Jen asked to be shown to her office. Francine got up a little grudgingly from her swivel chair (because of her nice hot cup of TEA), and took Jen down the corridor (fifteen) to a dark room full of old milk crates, golf clubs, *British Medical Journals*, a year's supply of substandard toilet paper, and several wheelchairs in need of repair. Was JEN supposed to repair them? She was about to ask, when Francine pointed languidly at a row of filing cabinets that lined the wall. She looked like a magician's Lovely Assistant drawing the audience's attention to her boss's interminable SCARF trick. Jen didn't at first take in the SIGNIFICANCE of the filing-cabinet gesture, but Francine soon explained that the filing cabinets were all in a muddle and it was Jen's duty to sort them out.

No one since MONICA LEWINSKY could have been less in the mood for filing. Jen had never understood a single filing SYSTEM. Her first MINUTE on the job, and already her total INCOMPETENCE had been revealed (and to a BEAUTICIAN!). For fear that Francine might run off and tell tales to Dr Lewis behind her back, Jen bustled her out of the room and, after an hour-long SULK, set to work.

Soon she was AWASH in paper. Folders cast their contents all over the room. The flood of paper neared the ceiling and threatened to ENGULF her: Jen was drowning in a RURAL BACKWATER! She needed the BREASTSTROKE just to get across the room to the cups of tea and coffee Francine kept bringing. These too needed filing! There were so many miscellaneous mugs lined up on the windowsill – some humorous ('Trust me, I'm a quack'), some dour ('*BMJ* – Read it Today', or 'it's all go with smithklineglaxo'), it was hard to tell which was the newest, fullest, and steamiest, without NUMBERING them.

For DAYS she filed and refiled and defiled (and reviled) pieces of paper Dr Lewis had amassed during just a few years in this rural backwater, reams of unpaginated patients' records and death certificates, questionnaires that patients had been forced to answer for no good reason, official complaints made by patients to the General Medical Council, tea-stained (or *tear*-stained?) ripostes sent by Dr Lewis to the General Medical Council, formal declarations of Dr Lewis's blamelessness sent back from the General Medical Council, recipes and postcards from patients, birthday and Xmas cards, photos of patients on holiday, articles torn from magazines on various subjects (medicine, cars, exotic foreign travel, massage parlours), and several free drug samples, long past their foist-by dates (Jen pocketed these).

At lunchtime every day, Jen would take her cheese sandwiches across the road to a bench under some trees and sit looking up at the surgery. She hadn't seen Dr Lewis since she'd started the job, though she'd heard his voice in the corridor (sixteen) occasionally, yelling at patients or Francine. He and Francine both seemed to disappear at lunchtime. Possibly TOGETHER. The thought filled Jen with unfathomable fury and despair.

The building that housed the surgery was a malevolent-looking structure, Gothic in intent, covered with turrets, widow's walks, and shutters that banged angrily in the wind. Jen often felt someone was STARING at her from one of the dark windows – it gave her the HEEBIE-JEEBIES (but then Jen ALWAYS felt someone was staring at her!). She had hoped that Francine would offer to give her a TOUR some time, but now she didn't WANT her to. Francine was a MURDERER, TORTURER, SLAVE-DRIVER. She was a ROMAN EMPEROR (Jen had read some Suetonius). She felt like WHOPPING Francine on the BUTT with that big greasy HANDBAG of hers, which Jen assumed to be full of foundation, concealer, mascara, lipstick, tweezers, emery boards, hairspray, travel irons, curling tongs, silicon BREAST IMPLANTS, stiletto-heel repair kits, beauty mags, cheek sparkles and PINK PLASTIC HAIR-CLIPS, as BARBIE's handbag would be. Any minute now Francine would start offering Jen beauty tips, and then Jen would have to KILL her. *I am going to have to kill you now.*

Beauty tips are always imminent for Jen. Nobody can quite BELIEVE anyone DARES look like Jen. That meandering flesh, the flesh of AGES, flesh of LEGEND, a SAHARA DESERT of flesh, were it all to be laid out in front of you end to end. A BROKEN landscape, a land of controversy and dispute, shaped by fire, flood, famine and feud (FOOD), its surface scarred, mottled, and punctured by CHASMS and suppurating sores. And yet, inside that blunt and bloated body is a mind that WORKS (sort of) – PLEASING to find in there something lithe and light that can leap and land on narrow ledges, a mind made wild by its own ideas!

Was she BORN angry? Nobody knows. What FEEDS her anger? MARS BARS? Maybe just having to proceed across the earth on THOSE LIMBS, and pay for things with shaky dimpled hands, sneered at by generation after generation of little sneering BOY.

Jen is like the FAT GIRL at school you befriend because she's fatter than YOU. You consider yourself KIND and want to score kindness POINTS, as well as securing a friend for life in the form of the FAT GIRL. She clings to you and you easily fall into the habit of letting her tag along after school to watch you smooch and smoke. It's all very HARMONIOUS until the day she turns on you and BLASTS you with your own REPULSIVENESS, suddenly revealing herself to be a MEZZO SOPRANO or GENIUS of some kind. When *you* believed she was truly pathetic and befriended her basically ON CONDITION she was pathetic. Afterwards you seek out other fat girls in a vague attempt to make amends until you finally give up, get a dog, and overfeed IT.

COELACANTH & CHIPS

It's like a day in CHILDHOOD before you realised everything SUCKS. There are BIRDS, BEES, and carpets of blue PETALS beneath blue bushes. SMALL carpets. DOORMATS really. But it's all WASTED on Jen! She rarely notices nature. There's a VEIL between Jen and the outside world that stops her seeing things. Instead, she is thinking about CARRIER BAGS. Jen is upset by the fact that everyone in the world now knows what a carrier bag looks like when it's full to bursting. MILLIONS OF YEARS of evolution have come to THIS: group awareness of the properties of PLASTIC. Most of the stuff we know, we don't NEED to know. Most of the stuff we know, we'd be happier NOT knowing.

To cheer herself up after work, Jen is on her way to the FISH SHOP. She wants FISH, and plenty of it! She has not tried the village fish shop yet. It looks like a lousy fish shop. In the window they have a few ancient crabs and pickled herring, and some beat-up plastic GRASS. But Jen is in the mood for fish. So she storms into the fish shop and is immediately confronted by two scary staring girls, painstakingly beautified. BEATIFIED. But how scary can they be, girls who smell of fish all day? Jen ploughs on with her plan and, looking one of the fish girls in the eye, asks if they have any cheap fish for CATS (her customary gambit in fish shops).

The fish girl just stares back at her, but not at Jen's face, at her FEET. OK, *OK*, I know, my socks have slipped down and are now bunched up inside my shoes, leaving my feet half bare, yes, YES? What am I supposed to DO, bend over right here and now and pull my socks up? Maybe you'd like me to kiss YOUR feet while I'm at it? I came in here for FISH – I didn't realise I was entering a fucking FASHION INSTITUTE.

STILL staring at Jen's feet, the fish girl walks over to the fridge, cold store, CHILL THING. It can't be a FREEZER because the fish in there still seems to be MALLEABLE! Yiiggghhhh! Malleable. It reminds Jen of that woman kissing her stuffed coelacanth. Were *its* lips once malleable?

The fish girl seems to be LIMPING. So maybe she takes a PERSONAL INTEREST in feet? But that still doesn't give her the right to stare so pointedly at MY feet. Maybe I don't WANT to be reminded of my SOCK problem all day. Maybe I want to be left in PEACE with my sock problem.

The girl hands over a small bag of whitish fish and says, 'Three pounds.'

'THREE POUNDS!?' exclaims Jen. 'Even if I *had* a cat, even if I had a cat I LIKED, I wouldn't pay that!' But in the end she hands over the dough, her hard-earned dough, taking care not to let the fish girl see her FINGER STUMP (the remains of the finger Jen caught in a car door when she was eleven). Don't want to give the creep anything ELSE to stare at! After all, could there be any better proof of INCOMPETENCE than a FINGER STUMP? Almost EVERYBODY has all their fingers! What must the DOCTOR have thought, who had to stitch me up? THIS CHILD IS AN INCOMPETENT, doesn't deserve good workmanship. Great STUMP, doc, thanks. Oh, and a wonky fingernail to go with it? PAY RISE FOR YOU.

Jen wants a whole COELACANTH now, all three FEET of it, blue-green scales and malleable sky-blue flesh quickly disappearing into her grey, flabby face. Jen never had a CAT, never had anything! Jen's life has been macabre, and it has made her melodramatic. She goes back to the flat and cooks her fish and a big load of OVEN FRIES to go with it.

SECRET EATING, the curse of all fat people. Eating normal amounts of PERMISSIBLE stuff in public (by the time you're THIS fat, that's only salad) while in private you eat all the BAD stuff, the stuff that should probably NEVER be eaten and therefore MUST be eaten, the fat person's CIVIC DUTY to syphon it all up, in revenge against the beauteous, the muscular, the moderate, the mincing, mediocre moralists, food experts and food ADJUDICATORS, the herbalists, the nutritionists, the misery-guts, spoilsports and PARTY-POOPERS.

Just THINK of all the cake and candy and ice cream and LUXURY MILK SHAKES and pizza and popcorn and Popsicles and potato snacks and chocolate brownies and macaroni cheese and tuna fish *AU GRATIN* that must be, IS, consumed in secret hidy-holes and hell-holes to compensate for all the HOLLOW eating performances of life, the whole eating CHARADE that life is! There's nothing BENIGN about secret eating, nothing jolly. It's OBSCENE, subversive, damn near CRIMINAL, and rightly kept underground.

Her RIGHT to be fat, her own BUSINESS if she no longer wants to be TOUCHED. Betrayals have formed her. Hungry for a place in the world, Jen eats. Hungry for contentment, containment, a little CONTINUITY, Jen eats. Hungry for sex, sedation, satisfactory SUNSETS, she eats. Hungry for beauty, grace, the GOOD things in life, MOSS, maroon, marbled halls, Italy, zebras, the moon, blue-green, Saturn, snow, peat fires, Fridays, autumn leaves, watery places and *La Traviata*, she eats. Hungry for CHEAP THRILLS, or the end of the world, she eats. Hungry for a mother's love, or the love of a good PSYCHOTHERAPIST, she eats. Hungry merely to be FILLED for once, fuelled for LIFE, Jen eats, she eats the food of TWENTY MEN (but why should MEN get it all?) and still it drains out of her and she needs MORE. She eats for the world, for the starving in Africa, and for herself alone, the many selves of her, the one she was yesterday and the one she'll have to be tomorrow. These selves stretch back in a long jagged line to her INFANT self: a fat baby.

A fat baby, left to roll around for hours on the rough fabric of the seat of an empty compartment after her mother jumped from the train – until Jen finally fell on her head and someone found her mewling and drooling on the floor. For this event, Jen has always felt vaguely BLAMED. She drove her own mother to suicide, drove her CRAZY. Jen has been trying to make amends ever since, by NEVER BEING HAPPY.

Through rape, secret eating, and emotional havoc, through being RIGHT and forever IGNORED, through being scorned and sneered and sniggered at, Jen has become the embodiment of female RAGE, a real STINKER, the eau de cologne of female MURK. For this she deserves awards, FOLLOWERS! Female rage, all twisted up into a barrelling CROISSANT of centrifugal force, is worthy of RESPECT.

In the ABSENCE of adulation, she wanks. Today, to her favourite fantasy of the RUSSIAN GUY ON THE TRAIN:

> A RUSSIAN GUY is sitting alone on a train. A young Englishwoman (Jen), gets into his compartment. They sit for hours in utter silence as the train zips through the STEPPES or the URALS or the CAUCASUS or somewhere. Finally, the young woman (Jen) asks if she could open the window a little. The Russian guy leaps up and says, '*Enough of zis talk! Take off your clothes!*'

An old joke, which Jen has elaborated on:

> Without preamble, without beginning or end, the Russian guy starts fucking Jen from behind while she looks out at the passing trees, the FORESTS OF RUSSIA. Jen is WEAK from his fucking but he doesn't care, he turns her and fucks her some more. He fucks her until all she KNOWS is his fucking (she's forgotten all about the trees of Russia!). All she can think about is his cock going into her, like a train in a tunnel. And by his intent expression she can see that all HE can think about is his cock going into her.

MEDICALLY IMPOSSIBLE

One day, Jen was summoned to Dr Lewis's office. It was their first real REUNION since she'd got the job. Beaming at her from his swivel chair, Dr Lewis told Jen that he was going to entrust her with some actual PATIENTS now. She tried to look enthusiastic. The next thing she knew she'd been sent back to her little office with her arms full of yet more PAPER!

Her new task was to write to all the women on Dr Lewis's list and persuade them to come in and have SMEAR tests. These are of dubious medical value and have an established record of failure, but Dr Lewis was going to get a big fat BONUS from the NHS if 50% of his women patients could be conned into having the test, TRIPLE if he could rustle up 80%!

Jen had to write a lot of LETTERS and lug them over to the post office. It took WEEKS. She wore out a whole pair of shoes, and was deeply, deeply bored. But the results were good: women started turning up in droves to have Jen shove her speculum up their fannies, pussies, beavers, slits, trims, twats, quims, gashes, snatches, purses, privates, kippers, cooches, boxes, DOWN-THERES, nether regions, undercarriages, WHATEVER they wanted to call it. The BUSH. Their RURAL BACKWATERS. (Most preferred the term FRONT BOTTOM – as if the cunt is just some miniaturised version of the ASS.)

Then they went home to await the worrying letters about

the results and the subsequent LAPAROSCOPIES and other unnecessary treatments for vaginal irregularities they didn't HAVE (Jen got all the SLIDES mixed up!). But it was WORTH it: the bonus was in the bag!

Jen's next assignment was to talk parents who didn't want their kids to have the MMR jab into LETTING their kids have the MMR jab. There were a lot of parents out there who were wary of the MMR vaccine, and Dr Lewis was SICK of them and their MMR worries. Who cares about AUTISM anyway? 'It's better than being DEAF,' as he said to Jen.

So Jen dragged the recalcitrant parents into her office, one by one (there wasn't much ROOM in there amongst the milk crates), and urged them to join the vaccination programme. 'Get with the programme!' she would tell them jocularly. Her technique was to deny, flatly, that there could ever be, or ever have been, any connection between the MMR jab and autism. It was 'medically impossible', she told them. Many parents were instantly persuaded by this – people want things to be medically POSSIBLE, that's just how they want the world to be!

But if they were still hesitating, Jen would badmouth the anti-MMR brigade: the campaigners and their so-called EXPERTS. She accused them of having ulterior motives in dissing the MMR jab, their true intention being to sell newspapers, or herbal remedies. These people were DANGEROUS, they wanted to cause an EPIDEMIC!!! She was SICK and TIRED of cowardly parents who sat back and let OTHER parents take all the risks. The *brave* parents, who had their children vaccinated, reduced the risk of measles in the COMMUNITY, from which the *cowardly* parents indirectly benefited . . . Bla bla bla.

If all else failed, Jen would say, 'I've had my OWN kids done! It's one's DUTY.' Nobody knew Jen HAD no children. Nobody knew who the hell Jen WAS.

Jen worked her ASS off to sell that vaccine, and discovered in the process how much Dr Lewis's patients DOTED on him. All she really had to say to most of the mothers was that DR LEWIS was keen on the MMR vaccine, and they would eagerly hand their kids over to Jen to jab. Wiping away a tear or a blob of blood afterwards, Jen would say, 'There now, you'll live!' and she was pretty much right: only a few kids died, two or three got autism, and NONE WENT DEAF. And Dr Lewis got another BONUS!

Oh, how the women of that rural backwater pined for Dr Lewis, longing to surrender themselves in every medically possible way to his stern stewardship. They were suckers for every skill, every pill he had to give (made out their WILLS to him too). They admired HIM, and through him, every echelon of his esteemed profession. These women wanted to be TAKEN OVER by modern medicine, looked at inside and out, orgasmically investigated, ROGERED till they felt no pain. He was like a MAGICIAN, wielding power over life and death with his magic wand. In fact, he could have been a FILM STAR with that CLEFT CHIN of his!

Men liked Dr Lewis too! Though he never went to the pub, and played golf on his OWN, if at all, he was revered at least for being WELL PAID. He was good about house-calls too. He sometimes turned up without even being ASKED, just to see how people were doing. He'd sit with his patient and have a nice big hot cup of tea, while he told gruesome medical stories, or expounded on bewildering aspects of the patient's condition, and bestowed upon it some Latin name. A bruise was not a BRUISE to Dr Lewis, it was an ECCHYMOSIS. His patients kindly ignored or at any rate TOLERATED the good doctor's own AKATHISIA (inability to sit still), his ECHOLALIA (parroting of his patients' words), his FASCICULATION (muscle twitches) and some outlandish BORBORYGMI (intestinal gurgles) – and luckily had no KNOWLEDGE of his TINEA CRURIS (crotch rot), PES PLANUS (fallen arches), or ZOOPHOBIA (which might not have gone down well in farming circles).

Ah, the strange primeval world of the medical man! Dr Lewis slept fitfully, and had dreams of TERRIFYING BLANDNESS. Nothing seemed to HAPPEN in these dreams: Dr Lewis would be wandering around some unfamiliar hospital looking for a place to WANK. Every time he thinks he's found a good spot, it turns out to be overlooked by a WINDOW opposite, or the wall beside him is a TRANSPARENT SCREEN, so he has to go off in search of somewhere better.

Most of these dreams occurred during brief naps in his swivel chair in the consulting room which despite the new paint job still smelled of pee, the age-old pee of PATIENTS. Patients can't seem to LOOK at upholstery without peeing upon it.

VAUDEVILLE

It was like fucking VAUDEVILLE in there!

PATIENT: I come about me *knee*, doctor.
It hurts when I bend it, and
I can't cross me legs no more.

DR LEWIS: Well, don't cross them! NEXT!

Never mind that a previously sound knee was now ON THE BLINK. That needn't interfere with the quick, easy, breezy, and CHEAP reply. Stomach hurts? Don't eat. Ass hurts? Don't sit/shit. Head hurts? Chop it off! Doctors will gladly CUT you up just to SHUT you up.

The thing about a rural practice is that you don't just treat one isolated person at a time. You treat MANY isolated people, all of whom happen to be RELATED. Dr Lewis prided himself on knowing their *names* – he memorised them at night. He also rehearsed his affable manner in front of the mirror – the gleam of his whitish teeth, the cold grey eyes – and honed his diagnostic skills by rummaging through the records of the dead, trying to remember what this or that incurable MOLE looked like, or the hot temper that accompanies a brain tumour. He took an INTEREST in his patients, of a sort.

MICHAEL was having trouble sleeping or concentrating. Dr Lewis handed him a big bottle of sleeping pills, saying, 'You'll be right as rain with these, Michael.' But Michael was having trouble sleeping because his wife had recently thrown him out of the HOUSE and told him she didn't love him any more. He had to make APPOINTMENTS to see his kids. He'd even lost custody of his DOG. Instead of hanging from a suspension bridge in a Spiderman outfit to demonstrate the indispensability of DADS, Michael swallowed all the sleeping pills Dr Lewis had given him and drove to a local beauty spot. Gulls danced and crapped on his car as he died.

Michael's daughter, JANET, was brought in to the surgery soon after this, weak, emaciated, constipated, and experiencing leg tremors when going up and down stairs. Diagnosis: inadequate food intake (she was STARVING). Treatment: cod liver oil. NEXT!

TREVOR was off to the BUSH on BUSINESS, and wanted a cholera vaccination. Dr Lewis made an innocent mistake that could happen to anyone: instead of a cholera injection he gave the guy MODECATE, a powerful tranquilliser. Trevor missed his flight to Africa and was found wandering around the airport in a disorientated state, having lost his testicles, spectacles, wallet and watch but – at least he didn't get cholera!

JAMES had just RETURNED from the bush (Malawi). His symptoms included fever and lassitude. Dr Lewis prescribed codeine. But four days later, James was no better. Dr Lewis had a flash of INSPIRATION and asked James if he'd taken any anti-malaria drugs before going out there. In his delirium, James thought Dr Lewis was saying 'anti-MALAWI drugs'. Of course he hadn't taken any anti-Malawi drugs before going to Malawi. That would be SILLY. James died two days later of cerebral malaria and renal failure. But he'd been quite wrong to suspect Dr Lewis of being ANTI-MALAWI.

JOHN had a sore hand. Dr Lewis sent him to hospital for an X-ray. They found that John had fractured a metacarpal, but it was well aligned so they left it unbandaged and told him to see his GP again in two weeks' time. Two weeks later, John duly went to see Dr Lewis. Proudly remembering John's name was *John*, Dr Lewis shook him warmly by the hand. They both heard a loud CLICK. When Dr Lewis released John's hand, there was now a very noticeable bump. John had to go back to hospital and have surgery on his hand. After that he was scared to shake hands with ANYONE.

SAM had a history of gout and came limping into the surgery with a sore foot. Dr Lewis prescribed more GOUT MEDICINE. The foot continued to deteriorate. Eventually Sam had to have his leg amputated below the knee: his gout was thereby HALF-CURED. Next!

IAN, a soldier home on leave, was spitting blood. Dr Lewis gave him some tablets. A few days later, Ian's distraught girlfriend SARA ran right past the flailing arms of Francine into the consulting room, where she begged Dr Lewis to tell her what kind of pills those were that he'd given Ian because SHE'D taken them: she had tried to commit suicide on account of Ian's imminent departure, but she'd had second thoughts. She now wanted to LIVE, and needed to know if she should go to hospital to have her stomach pumped. Unfortunately, Dr Lewis couldn't REMEMBER what the pills were, and hadn't made a note of it. Sara told him they were brown and shiny. Dr Lewis decided they must have been vitamins and told her not to worry. But they were NOT vitamins! They were IRON tablets. She died within the week.

JACK was a ninety-one-year-old with chronic CONSTIPATION. A humdrum affair. In fact his abdomen was swollen as tight and hollow as a drum! When Dr Lewis DRUMMED on it, there were strange CRUNCHING sounds. (Luckily, it didn't HURT him – Jack's Drum-Tummy was NUMB.) Dr Lewis sent him off with more senna pods. Jack eventually died of colonic cancer, which had blocked his bowel and made it BALLOON. Inside, they found hundreds of CALCIFIED FAECAL PARTICLES (and a hell of a lot of senna pods).

JOYCE, a five-year-old, had swallowed a drawing pin. Her parents kept bringing her in to the surgery because of her sore throat, but Dr Lewis couldn't see anything wrong until the *fourth visit*, when he noticed the drawing pin. This he removed but still Joyce didn't get better. She was listless and stopped eating. SPOILT, Dr Lewis concluded. Then she had a HEART ATTACK. In hospital, doctors discovered an ABCESS. They drained 40 ml of fluid from her windpipe, but she died anyway.

Dr Lewis killed people every day, people who wanted to live. Those that wanted to DIE, he saved. It's a system!

CATHERINE had motor neurone disease. Now unable to speak, she handed Dr Lewis a note she'd typed:

> Were I to reach a state of obvious misery and incapacity, leaving me wholly dependent on medication and the kindness of friends and relatives, I wish you to take no extreme measures to keep me alive.

Deeply offended, Dr Lewis declared, 'That would be a breach of my ETHICS, Catherine. I'm a good doctor! I passed all my EXAMS.' (He was always talking about those exams.)

MATTHEW, another patient with the same disease, begged Dr Lewis to keep him ALIVE, if only for a few months, so that he could finish a book he was writing on the Special Relationship between Britain and America.

'Of all the hare-brained schemes!' Dr Lewis said to him. 'People are always writing books! I can't spend all my time trying to keep them alive. Face it, Matthew, you're DYING. You have a FATAL DISEASE. Death is part of life. There's no getting around it!' By now, Dr Lewis was violently SHAKING the guy in his wheelchair. The little front wheels were spinning! It had been a long day.

He must have shaken him TOO MUCH. Matthew developed pneumonia. It could have been cured with antibiotics, if they had been administered quickly enough. Matthew's wife kept calling the surgery all morning, but because Dr Lewis was 'busy with the LIVING', he didn't come until the afternoon. By then, Matthew was dying. Dr Lewis was caught a little by surprise at this, and hurriedly called an ambulance, but it was too late: FOUR HOURS too late.

So the world never got to hear Matthew's inside knowledge of the chilling hold America has over Britain that results in Britain going along with every half-assed scheme of world domination America comes up with, the old SPECIAL RELATIONSHIP that would lead in the next few years to the deaths of hundreds of thousands of people (including IAN, incidentally). But Dr Lewis felt VINDICATED: Matthew did have a fatal illness. His death had proved it!

Another of Dr Lewis's more desperate patients was PAUL, who'd been on a RESPIRATOR for twenty years, after being paralysed from the neck down in a motorbike accident. For many years he'd wanted to die. He was taken care of by his old da, who now had cancer and only one leg. Dr Lewis dropped in on them every once in a while.

'What can I do for you today, Paul?' he would say, as he burned his tongue on one of their boiling hot cups of tea.

'Switch the respirator off,' pleaded Paul.

'Oh, you don't really want me to do that, Paul. What would your father do without you?'

'It's KILLING him, having to take care of me!'

Dr Lewis handed Paul some more painkillers and gave his father a nice pat on the back. Sometimes that's all patients really NEED: a good pat on the back!

Paul's father died a few months later. Paul was deposited in a nursing home where no one talked to him for weeks at a time. Eventually a cleaner accidentally turned his respirator off while hoovering the room, and that was the end of Paul.

ANGIE, the local postmistress, idly remarked one day to Dr Lewis, while getting him his Child Benefit money and a bag of sweeties (for HIMSELF, not his kids!), that she'd like as pain-free a death as possible. He told her to make an appointment. So a week or two later Angie appeared in the surgery. Dr Lewis had her lie on the couch and injected her with a plentiful amount of lidocaine. Then he pulled a curtain and left her to DIE, while he saw other patients!

At the end of the day he phoned Angie's niece, SYLVIE, and told her to arrange for an undertaker because Angie had 'PEGGED OUT' in the consulting room. Sylvie burst into tears and, in her confusion, started to babble about how she wasn't really Angie's NIECE but her GRAND-NIECE.

'I haven't got all day, Sylvie. Busy doctor, you know. Get a grip on yourself,' he sighed. 'Just tell me what you'd like me to put on the death certificate as the cause of death.'

Perplexed, Sylvie replied, 'Well, whatever she DIED of, I suppose!'

'OK!' Dr Lewis said cheerfully and hung up. His little joke.

PURE VAUDEVILLE.

ROGER LEWIS'S BODY

As a child he tortured goldfish from a fair, threw them on the ground to watch them squirm. But bones grow, a boy's bones. They MUST. Soon to handle the stretch to vagina, mortgage, taxman, grave.

In a sunny room at university he quickly climbed out of his clothes. His first love! Their paths crossed, criss-crossed, wound round. He has loved no one since.

He's proud of his long legs, neat hips, blond locks, grey eyes, cleft chin. Dr Lewis is well aware of the importance of his chin cleft to the VILLAGE. He shaves his sideburns so as to give EMPHASIS to his chin cleft, shaves them into POINTS that point at his CHIN CLEFT. He spends most of his TIME trimming those things! When not seeing patients or reading a magazine on exotic foreign travel, he's ploughing the field of his face.

The cleft in his chin has ECHOES elsewhere. You can't look at it without thinking of the groove between his BALLS, the crease down the middle of his six-pack stomach, his ass crack and the ridged and bumpy path of his spine. Taken together, these indentations are like an invitation to slice the guy IN HALF, by cutting along the dotted line.

People often describe the scrotum as outside the body, but it's not. If it was, you'd LOSE it! The scrotum is no more OUTSIDE THE BODY than an EAR is. Dr Lewis's scrotum is as firmly attached to him as anyone's is, and he (rightly) has no fear of losing it. But such fearlessness is a DENIAL of how soft and vulnerable the body really is. Men LIKE to deny this! Surfing, skate-boarding, sky-diving, hunting, mountain-climbing, drinking, driving and IN WAR, they fall for their own delusion of TAUTNESS. They seem to think the body is maintained through sheer will-power. Yet they die like everyone else when the planes fall and the bombs fly! Hell, they die falling off ladders fixing a LIGHT BULB. Mere flesh and blood after all, and mortal.

At a distant unisex salon Roger gets his highlights done. A blow-job from the sauna below. The mountains he's climbed for the sake of those hardened thighs! But does he KNOW what a ridiculous figure he is as he parades up and down the only real street in this rural backwater of his, hoping to be noticed by the GOILS? (No.)

His method of picking his nose, and blowing it, is unpleasant. But everybody, even ROGER LEWIS, has the right to handle his own body his own way. We're all at the MERCY of our bodies. We think we have free will but GLANDS pretty much tell us what to do. The mind is just one PIECE of the body. There's a lot of stuff we do WITHOUT thinking: breathe, swallow, play the piano, jerk away from HOT things. Men DUMP THEIR WIVES without thinking (Roger had). It's a sort of REFLEX ACTION.

WHAT'S IT REALLY LIKE TO HAVE A BODY?

A BIG RESPONSIBILITY! Always looking where you're GOING, trying not to get WET or RUN OVER. The best moments are mid-orgasm, or when you feel NOTHING. The rest of the time you're ON CALL, the caretaker doing the rounds, making sure everything's all right and you haven't blown a FUSE or something.

You register every sensation in case it means TROUBLE: odd vibrations, stirrings in the gut, a shrill ringing in the ears (or POPS or CLICKS, or a long BEEP), fleeting twinges in the wrist, knees or ankles, a BUZZING (?) in the genitals, blood, pus, blemishes of any kind. We live in constant fear of PAIN: kidney pain, breast pain, groin pain, abdominal pain, pain in the neck, pain in the ASS, headaches, earache, toothache, sore eyes, sore feet. And WEIRDNESS: sneezing, itching, oozing, twitching, throbbing, shrinking, swelling, collapses of any kind.

You spend a lot of time looking at OTHER PEOPLE'S bodies, FORGETTING your own. But it needs TENDING, so much tending! Having a body is a MASSIVE UNDER-TAKING. You try to keep it happy and healthy, warm or cool (according to taste), give it plenty of food, sex, baths, rest, haircuts. But it's such a PALAVER, no? All these NEEDS and FUNCTIONS and DESIRES. The body demands so much!

And then there's all the CLOTHING of the body that must

go on, since it's ILLEGAL or TABOO or at least EMBARRASSING to be naked. The body is an ANACHRONISM – we can hardly bear to admit that it exists! So out you go, traipsing your body round the shops to buy SHOES for it and undies and all the other stuff, the trousers, kilts and dresses, the jackets, ties and T-shirts, summer winter spring and fall. The *mothballs* alone required to keep this operation going! And then there's all the make-up and jewellery and deodorants you need to MASK the body (or show it off), the shampoo and nailclippers and nail varnish and nail polish REMOVAL PADS, the Elastoplasts and sunblock and soap, the pumice stones and SWARFEGA. The body is so NEEDY. How it LUSTS for its acne gel and ASSHOLE cream, its Pepto-Bismol. Sucks down its glucosamine and echinacea and vitamins by the score, and still it wants more!

The TATTOOS, the massages, the swimsuits, hats, coats, scarves, gloves and NAME-TAGS, and a mobile phone so you can be contacted wherever your stupid body happens to BE. Olbas Oil, Vick's Vapo-Rub, Q-Tips, Tampax, Kleenex, DEFLATINE. The products, PRODUCTS, designed to save you! Lumbar cushions too, iron lungs, artificial limbs, steel rods in the SPINE, new hips, new knees – it all adds up. Trusses, corsetry, condoms, bondage gear, stilettos six inches high in the heel! Asthma inhalers, defibrillators, sphygmomanometers, ultrasound scanners and X-ray machines. Padded INSOLES.

Fold-up stool, watercolour kit, binoculars, galoshes, thermos, camera, ACTION. A comb, a new TOOTHBRUSH every three months. Leather items. Nipple ornament of some kind. Car keys (CAR). House keys (HOUSE). Garden. Dog or cat. Tables, chairs, bed, TV, radio, CD player, COMPUTER, personal organiser (and/or SPOUSE). Kettle, stove, fridge, washing machine, ironing board (IRON), CLEANING AGENTS, pots and pans. Board games (BOREDOM), playing cards, Monopoly, chess set, piano perhaps. Stamps, envelopes, pens, pencils, scissors, Sellotape, recipes. A copy of *Jane Eyre*. Laundry basket (LAUNDRY), trash bags (TRASH), sticky sucky yucky stinky old rubber shower mat. Doctor. Lawyer. Vet for the pets. Thermometer. Loose change. Duvet. Doorbell. Egg cups. EYE CONTACT.

Without bodies, we wouldn't need trains or traffic lights, pavements or parachutes, mirrors or maracas! Many interesting HANDCRAFTS would have to go: lace-making, leather-embossing, tapestry, pargeting, Netsuke, embroidery, mosaics, bell-ringing, silver-smithing, quilting, smocking, SMOKING. Buttons would be of no further use. Ditto, DOWSING. It would be difficult, and POINTLESS, making risotto (all that stirring!).

Without bodies there would be no more telephones, marathons, triathlons, architects, wheelchairs, pilots, Pilates or prison! No PAPERWORK. No passports. No plastic surgery. No more so-called feminists going under the knife because they want their LABIA minimised. There would BE no feminists (no need!). No DESIGNER LABELS, no LOGOS – nobody left to ADVERTISE upon.

Without bodies we would no longer be subject to:

Momo syndrome
myalgia
arthralgia
thrombocytopenia
ascites
PANCREATITIS
peripheral oedema
sepsis
jaundice
comas
pregnancy
diarrhoea
pruritis

tinnitus
hypoaesthesia
alopecia
diabetes
deafness
sarcoidosis
palpitations
abdominal distension
cellulitis
mouth ulcers
pulmonary embolisms
vulvitis
dysgeusia
epistaxis
vasculitis
hyperglycaemia
epilepsy
dyspepsia
thyrotoxicosis
erythema
dysphagia
pancytopenia
ischaemic colitis
cholelithiasis
muscle cramps
abnormal gaits
dysarthria
haematuria
psittacosis
hepatic steatosis
papilloedema
cirrhosis
disorientation
dry mouths
dizziness

blurred vision
splenomegaly
gout
sinusitis
panic attacks
pollakiuria
hemiparesis
hypokalaemia
skin discolourations
erectile dysfunctions
encephalopathy
pleural effusions
tooth loss
hypoxia
multi-organ failure
bronchitis
eczema
urticaria
inflammations
mitral valve incompetence
constipation
restlessness
nasopharyngitis
BLUSHING
lethargy
mood swings
auto-immune disorders
TB
rhabdomyolysis
twitches
tics
blood potassium decreases
escherichia infections
retinal detachment
arthritis

diplopia
dysuria
skin lesions
angina
gastritis
psoriasis
thirst
pallor
haematemesis
demyelination
hypertriglyceridaemia
incontinence
reflux
ataxia
phlebitis
granuloma
photopsia
hyporeflexia
melaena
herpes
pericoccalsepsis
blepharitis
hypocalcaemia
hemiplegia
homicidal ideas
shock
abcesses
coagulopathy
CRYING
decreased libido
hoarseness
dementia
cryoglobulinaemia
cystitis
peritonitis

lichen sclerosus
aplastic anaemia
staphylococcal sepsis
hyponatraemia
hyperkalaemia
parkinsonism
tenderness
skin nodules
emphysema
glaucoma
aneurysms
cataracts
scotomas
hyperbilirubinaemia
metabolic acidosis
lipase increases
blindness
gynaecomastia
haemoptysis
myositis
ecchymosis
blisters
schizophrenia
polydipsia
burning sensations
rales
purpura
chromaturia
vitreous floaters
joint stiffness
attention deficit disorder
menorrhagia
paralysis
Guillain-Barré syndrome
mydriasis

thrush
cysts
lupus
pyelonephritis
flatulence
atelectasis
lacerations
depression
acute psychosis
tongue discolourations
faecal abnormalities
meningitis
mitochondrial cytopathy
piles
glossitis
Raynaud's phenomenon
atelectasis
tachycardia
pneumonia
vomiting
fibrosis
gallstones
gingivitis
stress
night sweats
rheumatic fever
goitre
empyema
electrolyte imbalances
hypothermia
azoospermia
vasovagal syncope
vaginitis
conjunctivitis
tunnel vision

tooth extractions
impetigo
spasms
Vogt-Koyanagi-Harada syndrome
hilar lymphadenopathy
eosinophilia
dysphonia
dysstasia
parosmia
nightmares
Sjögren's syndrome
agoraphobia
uveitis
contusions
scabs
HICCUPS
fluid retention
bursitis
mastitis
cyanosis
epididymitis
hiatus hernia
bruxism
bone spurs
venous stasis
chronic vegetative state
necrotising vasculitis
ureteric stenosis
DROOLING
tonsillitis
superior sagittal sinus thrombosis
carcinomas
tendonitis
skin odours
radiculitis

prurigo
HYDROCELES
spondylosis
carbuncles
choking
chalazions
cholangitis
anasarca
slipped discs
persecutory delusions
bone fractures
benign prostatic hyperplasia
haemarthrosis
arteriosclerosis
osteoporosis
typhoid fever
Basedow's disease
oesophagitis
Reiter's syndrome
gangrene
obsessive-compulsive disorder
nystagmus
paraplegia
ketonuria
irritable bowel syndrome
mitral valve prolapses
EUPHORIA
heat exhaustion
anaphylactic shock
wheezing
ventricular hypokinesia
self-mutilation
rhinitis
polyps
mesenteric vein thrombosis

personality changes
oliguria
keratoconjunctivitis sicca
iron deficiencies
marital problems
labyrinthitis
jitters
HEEBIE-JEEBIES
carpal tunnel syndrome
hirsutism
hypophosphataemia
exophthalmos
cachexia
crepitations
coeliac disease
chronic fatigue syndrome
barotrauma
ruptured arteries
scaly rashes
ototoxicity
oligodipsia
neurosis
nasal congestion
involuntary muscular contractions
Miller Fisher syndrome
metastases
menopause
lymphadenitis
intermittent claudication
lacrimation
ligament laxity
Stevens-Johnson syndrome
sprue
furuncles
Sick Sinus syndrome

ileitis
virilism
immobility
epiglottitis
despair
paroxysms
catatonia
rhonchi
intoxication
calcinosis
rotator cuff syndrome
pituitary tumours
plasmacytosis
oligohydramnios
obstructive uropathy
Ménière's disease
mumps
intestinal perforations
inguinal mass
Horner's syndrome
amaurosis fugax
excoriation
incoherence
galactorrhoea
anal neoplasms
membranoproliferative glomerulonephritis
gliosis
glossodynia
exanthem
anosmia
elliptocytosis
motor neurone disease
food intolerance
feelings of worthlessness
foetal distress

glioblastoma multiforme
club feet
corneal opacity
defecation urgency
diffuse large B-cell lymphoma
alveolitis
anion gaps
circadian rhythm sleep disorder
folliculitis
Mycobacterium avium complex infection
eructations
scabies
mononucleosis
febrile convulsions
diverticulitis
anhedonia
Alzheimer's
disinhibition
cryptococcosis
faecaloma
stiffness
Epstein-Barr virus
nocturia
motion sickness
vitiligo
toxoplasmosis
fungaemia
chorioretinitis
delusions of grandeur
endometriosis
SARS
microangiopathic haemolytic anaemia
vestibular neuronitis
transaminases
merycism

narcissism
miscarriages
telangiectasia
syphilis
portal vein occlusions
stridor
restless leg syndrome
metrorrhagia
chondrolysis
torticollis
sickle cell anaemia
snoring
sneezing
orchitis
CAT-SCRATCH disease
grunting
rectal tenesmus
subacute endocarditis
poverty of thought content
increased libido
lid lag
bone erosion
low Apgar scores
hangovers
aortitis
head-banging
iritis
leukaemia
obesity
tangentiality
staring
colonic fistulae
subileus
otitis media
lipoatrophy

Creutzfeldt-Jacob disease
bird flu
BINGO WINGS
formication
linophobia
sitophobia
taphephobia
scopophobia
silicosis
varicella
economic problems
clumsiness
neglect of personal appearance
purulent sputum
pertussis
sleep-talking
neutrophilia
sialadenitis
respiratory moniliasis
obliterative bronchiolitis
strongyloidiasis
orthostatic collapse
panniculitis
Klebsiella infections
asphyxiation
nonketotic hyperglycaemic-hyperosmolar coma
tumour lysis syndrome
haemosiderosis
haematochezia
being bedridden
osteitis
Palmar-Plantar Erythrodysaesthesia syndrome
pyromania
and GRASS BURNS.

There are bits of the body we're trained not to SEE, not to understand, different kinds of skin, flesh, flab. They don't register in blurry photographs of MODEL GIRLS – they've been airbrushed out or JOGGED to smithereens by the model herself or surgically excised or SOMEHOW obscured (a carefully placed PINEAPPLE perhaps). You have to study REAL people to get an idea what the body's really like. For the unobservant, this info comes in a series of SHOCKS throughout life. The way your stomach hangs when you lean forward, the sponginess of underarm flesh, the looseness of breast skin, cellulite, wrinkles, stretch marks – REVOLT US ALL!

We've been trained to view the body as a HORROR – not as a lovable, ESSENTIAL, egalitarian possession, but as a reprehensible, outrageous, superfluous thing we don't know how to HANDLE, unpredictable, guilt-bedecked, full of malfunction and mal-INTENT, an ENEMY that needs to be STOPPED, controlled: no flab, no flop. No pain or JOY either, no birth, no death.

We're being trained right out of EXISTENCE! With our RULES and our DIETS and our HEALTH SCARES and and TABOOS, our GYMS and our CELEBS, our FEAR and HATRED of the body, fear of SEX, fear of NAKEDNESS, and our love of PORN and GORE and DISASTER, our literature of GOOD-LOOKING GALS dabbling in APPEASEMENT – we've given up on OURSELVES! We've given up any moral claim we HAD on life. We're so full of regret and sorrow and foreboding and wistfulness, so full of SHIT, we've given up our right to our own bodies! Just waiting to be BOMBED really, mere units of energy and profit for capitalists and cloning.

FIRST-NAME TERMS

Jen, who WEEPS to see herself in the mirror, who will eat her own SHIT in prison, soon became accustomed to her normal daily routine. It was all nausea, palpitations, stiffness, itching, lumps, bumps, rashes, piles, breathlessness, dizziness, fainting fits, tics, twitches, swollen ankles, bleeding gums, insomnia, fatigue, lethargy, weight gain, weight loss, vomiting, diarrhoea, flatulence, high blood pressure, ominous skin blemishes, abnormal discharges, and depression. And that was just JEN!

She availed herself of all the technology at her disposal. She took her own temperature, checked her pulse, analysed blood, urine and stool samples, even got out the old STETHOSCOPE to listen to her lungs. She ascertained that she was feverish, her pulse racing, her breathing shallow. Searching through *101 Snap Diagnoses: The Lazy Doctor's Pocket Companion*, she settled on BRONCHOSPASM, pneumonia, emphysema, anaphylactic shock, or a BLOCKAGE due to plugs of thick MUCOPUS. But in the end she had to admit she was: IN LOVE.

It was his proximity in the building! Jen's senses were continually stirred by the sound of Dr Lewis moving around in the surgery, or in his flat upstairs. She listened out for his every BOWEL movement (the loo was right next to her office). She waited for the ring of instruments clattering to the floor of the consulting room, giving her an excuse to rush in and STERILISE stuff. She listened admiringly through the walls to the wails of his patients – Dr Lewis was not one to shirk or shrink from giving patients BAD NEWS. He was a doctor to his very bones: his words cut through people like a SCALPEL.

Jen had not intended to fall for another doctor. That OSTEOPATH at the hospital had fucked her like he was exploring OCEAN DEPTHS, fucked her hours at a time, his impassive face as blurry as the ultrasound images he recorded of their encounters. He'd driven Jen CRAZY with all that fucking, as crazy as she might have been if he hadn't fucked her AT ALL: the effect is roughly the same. It was a great relief to Jen when he just DISAPPEARED from the hospital one day, leaving his jacket on the back of a chair in his office, never to be seen again! (He was later found to have died HILL-WALKING in a thin shirt and work shoes – the urge to HIKE must have come upon him very suddenly.)

Despite her training (she had completed a six-week course on Infatuation) and her resolutions, but in accordance with doctor–nurse NOVELETTES, Jen had embarked on some serious hankering. She had always been a bit of a hankerer. She hankered for her next meal as soon as the last one was over! She hankered for PETS and PENTHOUSES and an adequate PENSION. She had hankered her whole life to have her MOTHER back. She hankered just to be a PART of things. Hankered and hankered, and hankered most of all for all the hankering to be OVER. But her feelings for Dr Lewis were quite unlike NAPOLEON'S for Josephine (Napoleon, according to JOSEPHINE, was easily QUELLED) – Jen's hankering was made of sturdier stuff.

They were now on first-name terms (though Jen still felt UNEASY about his name, especially the R in it). She liked the way his eyebrow quirked just before he told her to do something. She liked his trim waist and hips, his long legs, cleft chin, and his JAG. Jen LUSTED for his Jag. Sometimes

Woger CAUGHT Jen thinking about his Jag. He pretended not to notice she was thinking about his Jag, but the mere possibility that he might THINK she was thinking about his Jag made Jen UNCOMFORTABLE thinking about his Jag in case he thought she thought about it TOO MUCH. So instead she tried to think about HIS TAUTNESS in contrast to HER SOFTNESS (they were both extreme examples of their own body types).

But he was so ALOOF. He had clearly been HURT by some woman in the past! Jen had deduced this from the way he YOWLED in pain one day when she accidentally stepped on his foot. A less FRAGILE man might have smiled bravely and tried to FORGET the incident. But Woger seemed curiously OFFENDED. The usual indignities of life were UNENDURABLE for Woger. He had suffered, was STILL suffering, right down to his TOES.

One morning, Dr Lewis knocked on Jen's door and asked her what she was doing for LUNCH. Jen said she didn't know. The door shut. Jen sat there waiting for him to return. Maybe he would take her somewhere in his Jag! Maybe they would go to a cosy country PUB, as in doctor–nurse novelettes, and eat STEAK PIE and down a few pints and get a bit frisky in the back seat before returning to work (DUTY IS ALL).

But he never came back! The whole building went quiet, as it always did at lunchtime. Everything went still, RIGID. So did Jen! What finally roused her was her inability to BREATHE – she needed AIR! Gasping, she groped her way out into the corridor (twenty-three). Catching sight of the staircase, she suddenly hankered to be on the roof! Only there would she be able to breathe . . .

JEN SURVEYS HER DOMAIN

Plodding and panting up the stairs, Jen tiresomely aggrandises her sitch, comparing herself to a SLAVE, a CONVICT, a REVOLUTIONARY! Like Charlotte Brontë, Jen expresses her sense of injustice through HYPERBOLE, turning the slightest slight into a VIOLATION, the gentlest rebuke into a CURSE. It's a system!

Jen has lost sight of the true disappointments in life (they would overwhelm her), burying them beneath a MONOLITH of tiny ones she's blown up out of all proportion. She is daily burdened by bullies, strangers and MISCREANTS (patients). This is a woman who thinks in terms of TRAGEDY and TRIUMPH if she fails to extract money from a cash machine, or succeeds! This is a woman who feels browbeaten and disenfranchised if she runs out of BOG ROLL.

There is something absurd, is there not, in thinking in terms of LIBERATION just because you need some AIR? Something silly about constantly imagining yourself to be of intense interest to the POLICE, or to EXECUTIONERS. But like Brontë's, Jen's life has been macabre, and it has made her melodramatic. She has attempted to resign herself to her utter WORTHLESSNESS. But out of the fantasy of total rejection rises the phoenix of HEROIC RESCUE: Dr Lewis is Jen's designated Hero. As she stumbles past his door therefore she vows to subjugate herself to his will – her EMPEROR – if he will only free her from her CHAINS (and give her Wednesday afternoons off).

At the top of the stairs she unlocks a little door and steps out on to a very narrow balcony. She is instantly almost swept off it by the wind! But at least she can BREATHE. Jen surveys her domain. There's a huge chasm opposite the surgery, a purplish vulval VOID, surrounded by dark forested bluffs. She's noticed the local landscape is HILLY, but was unaware until now of such a dramatic DEPRESSION.

Cars zoom past below as she catches her breath. In one of them is a man who looks a bit like Jen's BROTHER. It is NOT her brother, but just the thought that it MIGHT be her brother is enough to revive Jen's sense of PERSECUTION.

People concentrate too much on PARENTS as the main influence on children. But what about a big bossy brother or sister who's always stealing your STUFF? Round and round you trail after this person who secretly DESPISES you and mourns those happy days prior to your existence. Nicky told Jen WHAT to do, and WHEN (never WHY), told her everything she ever knew or thought, told her she was ugly, mocked her body, mocked Jen's TENDERNESS too, mocked it until he KNOCKED it out of her; he criticised, deflated and defeated Jen at every opportunity.

For a time Jen believed there must be some LAW entitling older siblings to appropriate anything belonging to younger ones. Clothes, toys – even Jen's FOOD was never her own but subject to being swapped or SWIPED at any moment. All the dull TEDDIES given to motherless children were torn from Jen's arms and torn LIMB from LIMB by Nicky, yet Jen stuck to Nicky as if she too wanted to be torn limb from limb! All because Nicky knew how to steal from women's handbags, roll down hills without getting hurt, sleep outside in a tent, grate carrots, and rush little sisters to hospital when they got their stupid fingers caught in car doors (he had his MATERNAL side).

Nicky was Jen's BLUEPRINT for all future relationships, her repetitive search for love amongst SUPERIOR TYPES who were actually bent on her DESTRUCTION: all the SMART ALECS, ACHIEVERS, DECEIVERS, patronisers, bosses, ward sisters, RECEPTIONISTAS and misleading MOTHER FIGURES that badmouth her BEHIND HER BACK and always want to KILL her in the end.

She has never quite recovered from a sorry little incident at school. She and her supposed friends had had a big argument, and Jen had run off to the Girls' Loo to STEW. Her friends came in a few minutes later, unaware that she was there. Jen quickly hid in one of the booths, standing on top of a TOILET, like a JERK, so they wouldn't see her. It worked! From this precarious vantage point, Jen was able to spy on her friends and listen while they BITCHED about her:

'Well, I hate her!'

'So do I.'

'She thinks she's so special.'

'Teacher's pet.'

'She's ugly!'

'And stupid.'

'And FAT.'

'Did you ever see her in a swimsuit?'

'Ugh, no!'

'It's DISGUSTING!'

And so it went, for FIVE MINUTES. Jen hardly dared breathe, and it was tricky getting *off* the loo after they'd left, she was so STIFF. She's had no great faith in friendship since, though she can still be duped by the HEROIC and MARVELLOUS.

For years Jen has pursued such people, in the hope that somehow their glory will wash off on HER, and that she will thereby become WORTHY of them. But most of these people don't even notice Jen EXISTS! She is distant, they assume unfriendly when in fact she is merely suffering from

AWE. She liked Urma Thurb so much she wanted to jump up on her lap sometimes, lick her all over and kiss her on the MOUTH, like some kind of playful, passionate and spontaneous DOG. But the betrayals have mounted up, making Jen the stinky, slinky, doomed and reviled creature she is today, scuttling along her widow's walk like LONDONERS scuttled in their overcoats after the war. You see them in photographs, hollow and damaged, COLD – but still able to SHOP, read newspapers, PROCREATE. People carry on. It means nothing but they do. They survive stuff and proceed. Doesn't mean they're HAPPY.

Jen originally went into nursing to get *away* from Nicky, who'd done DENTISTRY. She didn't think their careers could possibly collide but she was WRONG. Doctors at the hospital were always coming up to her and asking if she was related to NICKY, the ORTHODONTIST, and if so, could they have his PHONE NUMBER. He was much in demand. Jen told them Nicky was just a DENTIST, but it made no difference! That was one of the reasons Jen applied for the RURAL-BACKWATER job – not much call for GOOD TEETH in a dump like this.

Jen paces to and fro on her widow's walk, working up her usual head of STEAM about her brother. She's particularly irked at the moment by Nicky's refusal to hand over Jen's share of the MONEY from the sale of the family flat, their MUTUALLY OWNED property. Nicky INSISTED on selling it and now he isn't handing over the dough. He still can't admit I EXIST. He thinks HE gets EVERYTHING.

Jen tried to scupper the sale! The day the viewings were meant to start, she crept out at dawn and pinned a notice to the front door:

DUE TO THE MURDER
AND ONGOING POLICE
INVESTIGATION, TUBA-

BAND PRACTICE WILL
TEMPORARILY BE HELD
IN FLAT DIRECTLY
BELOW, MONDAYS,
WEDNESDAYS & FRIDAYS.
DAILY REHEARSALS TO
RESUME NEXT MONTH,
ALL BEING WELL.
CHEERS!

(Jen had always wanted to play the tuba!)

Nicky couldn't understand why no one was coming to see the place until, in exasperation, he flung open the front door and found a HAGGARD-LOOKING COUPLE out on the landing, peering at the SIGN. With great aplomb, Nicky tore the notice off, guffawing merrily, and managed to steer the blasted pair inside. So now HAGGARD-LOOKING PEOPLE snooze in Jen's old bedroom (it was the biggest – and Jen had grown to fill it) while JEN penuriously poultices the impetigo of the local peasantry –

Her train of thought is abruptly halted by a loud QUACK. It sounds like a homicidal CROW, or GOOSE, or maybe a COW (Jen's not too up on her animal noises). She hears it again and spins round, nearly falling off her perch. What's SQUAWKING? Then she realises it's coming from INSIDE the house, and it's LAUGHTER. Somebody's LAUGHING at her! Can it be Dr LEWIS, chortling over Jen's outrage at not being taken out to lunch?!

Jen doesn't like being LAUGHED AT, any more than she likes people talking about her BEHIND HER BACK. Even when people talk KINDLY about her – as Urma Thurb often did during shift changes and weekly managerial meetings – the mere THOUGHT of being talked about makes Jen CRY. Mortified and furious now, INFLATED by fury, Jen finds it quite hard to squash herself back through the little door. The laughter, if it can really be CALLED that, seems to be coming from Dr Lewis's flat, as Jen tiptoes past. Her pace accelerates as she rushes down the stairs, a whirling fury BALL, to her dungeon. Slamming the door behind her, she falls down the steep steps in the dark. She HOPES she's sustained a serious injury, necessitating Dr Lewis's immediate assistance – but she has merely BRUISED herself all over, and has to CRAWL into the kitchen to microwave herself some PIZZAS, which she washes down with lots of LOW-CAL WHITE WINE, thinking as ever about Nicky's SCORN for her occasional dieting efforts (such as dry white wine). Then she lugs herself like a wounded ANIMAL, into her bedroom, and flops on the bed.

Above her, hanging on the wall, are dozens of HAND-BAGS, bulging like SKIN CELLS under a microscope. Each a different size, colour, texture. Such VARIETY: this must be what MEN want, Jen thinks, THIS is what they require of women: they want a different size, colour, texture, personality, a different PERSON, every day! What are the chances she'll ever hit the day Woger wants HER?

She weeps until her den looks as red to her as a fox's lair and Jen herself is MAROON, marooned there on damp blankets, nursing her full stomach and sore wrist, waiting for something GOOD to happen. She falls asleep at last and dreams about Dr Lewis, dreams he's TINY! She watches as he gets into a tiny CAR and drives along the PAVEMENT, a dangerous thing to do when you're that small.

PANDORA'S BOXES

Yes, Jen had finally unpacked all those pesky BOXES. They weren't full of clothes or books or HEIRLOOMS (the only thing Jen had inherited was her unfortunate ATTITUDE). Of course, she had the usual copy of *Jane Eyre*; also, an old Dionne Warwick tape. She had her fair share of PASTA pots and frying pans too, a few toiletries, towels, some colourful little rugs, nursing textbooks she had never read and never WOULD read, and a very small CACTUS which may or may not have been DEAD.

But most of Jen's boxes contained one item only: a handbag. Jen liked RETICULES. She even liked the WORD 'reticule' (she was alone in this). Her handbags had been packed resentfully and with care, their confinement excusable only on grounds of privacy. Jen's handbags were not for everyone's eyes!

Women like things that OPEN. They like CONTAINERS. They like soft, rounded, glinting secret things with colourful folds suggestive of something PRECIOUS. Oh COME ON, they like anything resembling a CUNT. Men have their phallic ties, women their labial handbags.

In the STONE AGE, women didn't NEED handbags, not just because they didn't have any money, keys, lipstick or cigarettes, but because they could show off their actual GENITALS. They were NAKED for chrissake! The pursed lips of their cunts were on display ALL DAY.

Clothing, and being UPRIGHT, interfered with LORDOSIS and the easeful exhibition of female genitalia. Cunt SUBSTITUTES had to be found, cunt ADS. The cunt itself went into hiding! These have been the cunt's WILDERNESS YEARS. How inconvenient that WHOLE HUMAN BEINGS emerge from this void. One of the most absurd achievements of human civilisation has been to drain the cunt, the CUNT, of meaning. People are always draining things.

Hence, the handbag. Worn on the arm, held in the hand, strapped over the shoulder, attached to the waist (the 'fanny-pack'), or hung on the back in the form of a mini RUCKSACK (displacing all sexuality to the rear), the handbag is an awkward thing to carry, prone to loss or theft. A POCKET might be more secure. But a pocket doesn't convey a lifetime of one-night stands, disaffection, or your readiness for LOVE! For a handbag is not just a vehicle for transporting your make-up, your chequebook and SWEETIES. It's an emblem of your VAGINA.

Many believe handbags convey something of the actual CONTOURS and CHARACTERISTICS of their owners' sexual anatomy! Yet so many women remain unconscious of the expectations they raise with a nice plump soft jingly jungly rounded and ridged spectacle of a receptacle, that snaps open at the lightest touch. Nor do they seem aware of how easily desire may be NULLIFIED at the sight of a zippered waterproof leathern BOX, pockmarked with tiny CRATERS like inverted nipples (but they SHOULD be).

Some handbags have openings you can't get your HAND into. These are not happy handbags! Handbags want to be rooted through, manhandled, they want their bottoms searched, they want to be fondled, fingered and FILLED. No doubt about their ultimate aim: impregnation. Handbags crave contents.

There are people who see words as COLOURS. These

people are EXTREMELY TEDIOUS and never more so than when they're talking about their FUCKING SYNAESTHESIA. What do they MEAN, green is the colour of Wednesday? What the hell are they TALKING about, and why do we let them get AWAY with it? Jen didn't see words as colours, I'm glad to report, but she did see women as HANDBAGS. Whenever she met a woman, she would study the woman's handbag to assess her PERSONALITY. Hard-assed rectangles of stiffened QUILTING for the heartless; round iridescent magnetic sacs for the hapless and helpless. Tiny shiny hand-held PODS for flighty ice maidens; galumphing CARPET-BAGS for the jilted and jaded, the faded, the chlamydia-invaded. Softies seek out handbags of feather, felt, silk or straw. Others more predatory choose alligator, leopard-print and pony pelt. (Poor ponies!) The monogamous favour BUCKLES.

Nobody has HOBBIES any more, but handbags were Jen's hobby. Sometimes she perhaps expected TOO MUCH of a bag! She still had one of her mother's: navy-blue with a gold-chain handle. Jen had searched it for TRACES of her mother, of which there were none, apart from a half-used powder compact. In an inner pocket, there was a matching navy-blue leather-backed MIRROR, that Jen looked into once in a while to see if she could find her MOTHER. (WHAT? Wouldn't you?)

But much of her collection had been amassed by STEALING the handbags of old ladies at the hospital during difficult days on the Geriatric Ward. When Jen didn't like somebody, she took the old duck's handbag home and ABUSED it, voodoo-style, stabbing it with SCISSORS or SHITTING in it or twisting it into a tight unseemly BALL. (She NEEDED to do this, for her own sake and that of OTHERS, or rage might have OVERWHELMED her!)

She never stole the handbag of a woman she ADMIRED. Instead, she would ASSIGN her a handbag from the preexisting supply or, if necessary, BUY her a nice handbag (that the woman in question would sadly never see!). Into it, Jen would then tuck HONORIFIC OFFERINGS – perfume, ciggies, flowers, autumn leaves – and messages of praise (sometimes tempered by a few words of COMPLAINT or PERPLEXITY if the friendship wasn't going too well). Every handbag Jen owned represented some imaginary friend or enemy or other.

She had one she'd selected for URMA THURB: dark-blue corduroy with yellow suede trimmings. Inside, Jen kept an old Kleenex that had a lipstick imprint of Urma Thurb's MOUTH, Urma Thurb's lost earring, a cherished example of Urma Thurb's handwriting: a prescription Urma Thurb had written for some VINCRISTINE (which Jen, in a fit of pique over something Urma Thurb had said, injected into a child's SPINE, with catastrophic results), a photo of Urma Thurb standing beside the Falls at Killin on her honeymoon, and white nurse's socks that Jen believed had once belonged to Urma Thurb. This was the handbag Jen most often slept with.

Jen's own handbag was very large, capable of carrying SO MUCH. How readily it opened to gape and gulp emptily at the air. Like a big FISH it floundered, often vomiting its contents at the worst moment! Every day, she stuffed it with cheese sandwiches (or tuna fish), a couple cans of lager, a copy of *Nurse Prescribing*, a few spare syringes, deodorant, air freshener, tampons, safety pins, cookies, chockies, ciggies, bickies, keys, her wallet, some socks in case she was cold, a piece of cardboard to use as a fan in case she was hot (more likely), and baby powder for her chafing thighs and the airless acres under her breasts (Jen smelled more like a BABY than she ever realised).

But it could have held much more!

XMAS PUDDING

May and Marvin Eakins, so NICE, so normal, so comfortable with themselves and the way they DO things, so content and contained in their snug little bungalow next door to Dr Lewis's surgery, with their bevelled glass mirrors, their gigantic WARDROBES, their silver brush-and-comb sets, their doilies, the telephone on its telephone TABLE, their childlessness, their bill-paying promptitude, and the two-person BURIAL PLOT mown weekly in advance.

SO pleased are they with all this, they are continually ASTOUNDED by OTHER people and the way they organise themselves! A lone woman eating a sandwich in the PARK earns their stares, since she's eating ALONE and her COAT is dragging on the ground (also, they have no idea what KIND of sandwich she's eating). A man walking by surprises them because his hair's longer than MR Eakins's and he's walking FAST – faster than either of the Eakinses has walked for DECADES. A JOGGER passes. His hair is SHORTER than Mr Eakins's. They observe his steamy breath with consternation, barely able to comprehend what it IS or how it GOT there. It EMBARRASSES the Eakinses that this fellow is steaming up the park.

They're particularly stunned by the way other people handle DEFECATION. The Eakinses sit on their respective toilets in public loos listening in DISMAY and ALARM to the bodily functions of others and wincing at the sight of alien pubic hairs or yellowish DRIPS on the seat. The horror, the HORROR! In fact, anything anybody does, be it WALKING, SITTING, EATING, SNEEZING, YAWNING, SLEEPING, KISSING, FARTING, PISSING, SHITTING, FUCKING, THINKING, BLINKING, or VOMITING (all the things people do in more or less THE SAME WAY), serves as a source of wonderment, worry and regret for the Eakinses, an excuse for staring OPEN-MOUTHED at the time and commenting upon later at home.

The Eakinses moved to the country to enjoy their OLD AGE, but it's getting less and less enjoyable. Even popping down the road to the shops or the bank is a burden and a challenge. The TOTING of stuff. The body in old age is like a teenager who needs to MOVE OUT: it starts making TROUBLE until you're glad to be rid of it. This is the process the Eakinses have embarked on.

May Eakins has always assumed that Marvin loves her a little more than she loves HIM. This, she feels, is the recipe for a HAPPY MARRIAGE. She has kept him on his TOES by always being a tad REMOTE – through this, and never wearing YELLOW, May has retained her mystery. But secretly she *prides* herself on Marvin and has served him loyally. In the old days she threw many a party for Marvin and his cronies, who would become flirtatious on sherry and luncheon-meat. May turned down many men who might have loved her MORE. For MARVIN, she entirely missed out on the BUSH.

Instead, she darned his socks, ironed his newspapers, erected windbreaks on rainy beaches (while Marvin inspected tide pools), and regularly sent his suits out to be cleaned. For Marvin she's shaved her armpits for FIFTY YEARS. She has also permitted carnalities, of a fairly muted order, and has paid for his Xmas presents from interest on her own SAVINGS.

In return, Marvin DOES love May a little more than May

loves him! He is immensely concerned for May's welfare and happiness and likes to PAMPER her, fetching a shawl or the PEANUTS, even if they're closer to May. He's interested in everything May has to SAY, and agrees with her whenever possible. He is ENTHRALLED by May, convinced of her good taste and intellect. If May wants chintz curtains, she GETS 'em. When she says it's time for Shepherd's pie, he EATS it!

Linked lovingly in abstention from almost EVERYTHING, they have established a harmonious little life for themselves, their only worry: who will DIE first. The one who loves the most, or the one who IS loved? It doesn't make much difference. You don't give your WHOLE LIFE to someone without losing track of what you'd do on your OWN. For YEARS they have hidden in fear of this event, peering out, between the chintz and the chats, at peculiar characters, and the savage storm to come.

One morning, a CAR drove right across their carefully manicured front garden and hit the side of the Eakinses' bungalow! The driver of the car died. The Eakinses were unhurt, but the police arrived and declared their house UNSAFE: the Eakinses had to be EVACUATED! The police offered to take them to hospital, but, fearing the chaos of the indiscriminately sick, the Eakinses said they would prefer to go next door to the GP's surgery.

Arriving with a POLICE ESCORT at least ensured that the Eakinses got past FRANCINE. But she told them the doctor was OUT – they would have to go see the new NURSE. The Eakinses smiled gratefully and were led by Francine along the corridor (fifty-seven) to Jen's grotty little office.

The Eakinses had so far been SPARED any encounter with Jen, and even though she wasn't doing anything much, just sucking a lollipop and reading *Jane Eyre* with her feet up on the table, the mere sight of her (which unfortunately included a glimpse of KNICKERS beneath her white nursy hem) caused Mr Eakins to FAINT and Mrs Eakins to have a panic attack!

Francine and Jen had to carry them both into the consulting room and lay them on the couch (they were so SMALL they could both fit on, arsy-versy). Then Jen sat with them, trying to calm HER and revive HIM. The trouble was, every time MR Eakins woke up and got another look at Jen, he conked out again, flopping backwards against MRS Eakins, whose BREATHING difficulties then increased! This push-me-pull-you routine might have gone on FOR EVER, had not Dr Lewis returned at last and, upon examination, declared that Mr Eakins was essentially OK, but Mrs Eakins had had a STROKE, brought on by the shock of having a car drive into her house. (Only JEN knew that the shock was not the CAR CRASH but seeing JEN.)

Every Xmas of their lives together, the Eakinses had dutifully lit a Christmas pudding that oozed and flopped and fumed like Jen's ASS. Stiffened and boiled in a PUDDING CLOTH, Jen's rich dense brandy-soaked ASS seemed a mockery of DEATH, a CANNONBALL from the glorious colonial past, emblem of EMPIRE. On some level, May and Marvin Eakins had always believed that eating Christmas pudding was a PATRIOTIC ACT that might eventually SAVE them from death!

But those puddings were so ROTUND, so complex, so full of SUET, they were an OUTRAGE. Eating them was an act of SABOTAGE against the modern era and DECENCY itself! It was like spooning up Jen's PUSSY into their innocent mouths, STUFFING themselves with malign and malodorous MISHAP. That pussy-footing pudding somehow contained their DOOM, their downfall (and no sixpence).

FOOTBALL

Dr Lewis had an innocent love of football which had only led to a few fatalities so far. He had a TV in the consulting room. His patients were very impressed by Dr Lewis's ability to prod their pimples and piles, and scribble out a more or less legible prescription, without taking his eyes off the game.

Today, Barcelona was playing against Paris St Germain for the final Cup in the final Cup Final of the European Cup Winners' Cup Final FINAL, and Dr Lewis didn't want to miss it! But MARTHA arrived, a new patient, who was suffering from CONTINUAL ORGASMS. Anything that VIBRATED set her off: riding on a bus, a bicycle, showers, loud DRUM beats and bass notes, hoovering, BEETHOVEN, even getting too close to an active WASHING MACHINE. Masturbation brought only temporary relief: Martha was EXHAUSTED. She was just an orgasm MACHINE, a SLAVE to the antics of her clitoris! This was Dr Lewis's first case of involuntary orgasm syndrome. He decided to see her DAILY, for electrotherapy, hydrotherapy and massage. He just hadn't decided who would massage WHOM yet! (*Baboom-tttzzz!*)

Now it really was time for the GAME. Dr Lewis shooed Martha out but as soon as he turned the damn TV on, he got an emergency call to attend an OBSTETRIC crisis some place miles away! Irritably collecting his coat, medical bag and NURSE, Dr Lewis stormed out of the surgery and drove

TOP SPEED towards the CRISIS, crackly football coverage on FULL BLAST.

Jen didn't know what was the MATTER with him, he seemed so preoccupied (she was unaware, as yet, of his devotion to football). He didn't say a single word to her throughout the journey! But – at least she was finally in that JAG.

When they reached the remote cottage, they could hear SCREAMING. 'Might need an ambulance,' said Dr Lewis cheerfully, hoping he might be able to get back home for the game after all. But when they examined the woman, it was clear that there was no time to lose: it was a BREECH birth and the baby's legs were already hanging out!

Jen organised the rubber gloves, sterile pads, local anaesthetic and scalpel, and Dr Lewis was just about to start the Caesarean when he paused, looking about as if he'd lost something.

'Margaret,' he said. FRIEDA didn't respond. 'Frieda, I mean. Where's your TV?'

'TV?' mumbled Frieda, nearly delirious from the pain. She nodded towards the window. Dr Lewis quirked urgently at Jen, who went over to the window and, sure enough, there was a small TV set! Dr Lewis got her to drag it closer so that he could watch the game whilst operating.

He cut through several layers of Frieda's skin, muscle, and her abdominal sac, and was about to TEAR her womb open with his bare hands (as was his custom) when a GOAL was scored by Paris, or Barcelona, or Brussels or Luxembourg or LUXOR – whichever team it was that Dr Lewis was rooting for. The knife *slipped*, and the baby's cheek was cut. But Frieda was so pleased the kid was ALIVE, she made no comment on the knife wound! And Dr Lewis got to see his preferred team win the game, so all was well.

Jen stitched the baby's cheek and tidied up a bit while they awaited the ambulance that would take Frieda and the baby to hospital to recuperate from their respective OPERATIONS.

On the way back to the surgery, Dr Lewis seemed ELATED, whistling away to himself!

'That kid'll be right as rain,' he told Jen, 'as soon as he's old enough to grow a beard.'

Jen, relieved that he was SPEAKING to her at all, didn't bother reminding him the baby was a GIRL.

CATHETERISED MARES

Roger Lewis would never have designed things this way, he would never have put WOMEN in charge of reproduction! Women are the source of all misery! This was why he'd gone into MEDICINE. To control women and death: these were his humble aims. (He'd passed all his exams!)

Dr Lewis dreamt of a better world where the PENIS would be given preference (and its statistically rightful amount of GP TIME) over all the meaningless leakages of women, who seemed in constant need of being DRAINED. Dr Lewis dreamt of a better world in which liquids were only emitted AT WILL. He denied ABSOLUTELY that there was anything INTERESTING about being female, that MENSTRUATION for instance is INTERESTING. For Dr Lewis, if men don't do it, it must be VILE.

And women make such a FUSS, every day a new fuss-wuss! He'd recently done a D & C on some goop who desperately wanted a baby (the D & C was supposed to help her conceive). Was it HIS fault the woman was pregnant ALREADY? OK, he forgot to do a pregnancy test before embarking on the procedure but, APART from that, was it Dr Lewis's fault that there happened to be a thirteen-week foetus in there, which he'd then had to drag out piece by piece? It was an HONEST MISTAKE that ANYBODY could have made! (More bits came out by themselves over the next few days.)

He'd given another woman, AT HER REQUEST, an abortion in her own HOME – what could be more convenient? But she too was dissatisfied! Just because he'd wrapped the foetus in a TOWEL, which somehow ended up in the LAUNDRY pile – the scrawny corpse went through two hot washes and a SPIN before the woman found it. But what did that have to do with Dr Lewis? Busy man. Couldn't be everywhere, TIDYING and whatnot.

Dr Lewis had a lucrative little sideline as a MEDICAL EXPERT on Mental Health panels, particularly in cases of frequent *miscarriage*. In Dr Lewis's opinion, one miscarriage is normal, two suspicious, and three MEDICALLY IMPOSSIBLE and a clear sign of MUNCHAUSEN'S SYNDROME – the woman must have secretly obtained an abortion and claimed to have had a miscarriage in order to draw ATTENTION to herself (women are WEIRD). Dr Lewis had arbitrarily estimated the chances of a woman having three miscarriages in a row as one in TWENTY-THREE MILLION.

Everyone on the Mental Health panels was much TAKEN with this estimate (it had a nice ring to it), and many a miscarriage-prone missy had been unceremoniously slotted into a STRAITJACKET on Dr Lewis's say-so. He was well-paid for his testimonies! (He was expecting an OM any moment!) The fact that twenty-three just happened to be his FAVOURITE NUMBER was something Dr Lewis chose to keep to himself.

But now one of the silly women he'd helped to diagnose was threatening to SUE! Not just for her lengthy hospitalisation (during which she'd been attacked repeatedly by PRO-LIFE inmates), but also for the two years she'd lost with her existing children and her husband, who was now SUICIDAL. She'd be suing Dr Lewis if her TOILET didn't flush next! She'd even dared to cast doubt on the 23,000,000 thing. Women are such QUIBBLERS.

His heart now sank to see VIRGINIA hobbling into the consulting room: an American, with an American's predilection for learned discussions of SYMPTOMS (she had even asked once for a thorough CHECK-UP, whatever that was). She had come to him months ago about the menopause. It hadn't really STARTED yet, she was PERI-menopausal, but Dr Lewis had given her a huge supply of HRT anyway, and the requisite lecture on the redundancy of the human female after fifty.

'In ancient times, Virginia, you'd be DEAD by now,' he'd told her, quirking steadily. She'd gone off much reassured, no doubt. (He was ALWAYS talking about those ANCIENT TIMES! He loved to think about the human in the WILD, coping without a GP.)

But here she was, back again, complaining of fainting spells and a new pain in her left leg, which she claimed was PURPLE. On examination, Virginia's assessment of the colour of her own leg proved CORRECT. She was also bleeding profusely (from the vagina, not the leg), and had CHEST PAINS. It was endless! She should have booked FOUR appointments. Worst of all, she had made up her own mind already about the diagnosis! How Dr Lewis hated self-diagnosis: it robbed him of all his FUN. Virginia, it seemed, had decided all her problems stemmed from the HRT she was taking. An absurd idea.

'I'm not sure I even NEED hormone replacement yet. I think it's making me really SICK, and isn't it made by harvesting pee from permanently immobilised, catheterised mares? That is a lot of animal torture for something that isn't even a DISEASE.'

JESUS, you give a woman a WONDER DRUG and all she can do is BEEF about it. 'We use animals for many things,' Dr Lewis began.

'But the menopause is NATURAL. Why do I have to take medicine for it?'

Dr Lewis spent the next FIFTEEN MINUTES assuring Virginia that none of her symptoms could have been caused by HRT, all the time wondering how Francine would fob off his next patient. Finally, just to get Virginia OUT of there, he took a chance and felt her breasts for lumps and *found* one (caused by HRT!). What luck – this was a matter for SPECIALISTS. He informed Virginia gravely that he was referring her to the hospital for tests and she would probably require a mastectomy.

'Not without a second opinion,' she declared, before starting to cry. Oh, TEARS, yes, Dr Lewis's schedule had been ruined by many a woman's tears.

'What CAN you be crying for, Virginia? Most women readily accept the loss of a breast!'

More crying! Women get so ATTACHED to their bodies. He was SICK of it, the endless cavalcade of women who trooped to see him, each one trying to preserve her own little expendable frame. No BEAUTIES any of them!

'Go home and talk to your husband about it, Virginia. I'm sure he'll agree with me.'

Virginia gathered her clothes and rushed out of the room. Roger was at last able to relax. There WERE no other patients in the waiting room, as it turned out – he had panicked quite unnecessarily. So he got out a magazine on exotic travel destinations (Dr Lewis had big travel plans, so far entirely unfulfilled), and was soon contentedly fantasising.

Thus, everything NATURAL in women, Dr Lewis treats as sinister, unnatural, and disastrous; everything UNNATURAL (like drugs, or premature DEATH), he treats as NATURAL. It's a system!

HE HAS ALWAYS DONE THIS. He has always bored, manipulated, deprived and abused women! He has no RESPECT for them, even his own DAUGHTER, whom he drives MAD with guilt and worry. She worries about HIM, how ALONE he is, how defeated, how pathetic, how hard he works, how hard-done-by he is, how the WHOLE WORLD OWES HIM A LIVING, how everyone he's ever known has either PEGGED OUT or let him down some other way. He complains to her about his FINANCIAL difficulties until she's ready to go on the GAME to help him (and she's only *twelve*).

His long lectures! But he CHOSE to live like this! He CHOSE his sordid existence. He has recklessly thrown away his chances in life, his middle-class upbringing, his stable-enough childhood. (He never passed those EXAMS: he was taking too much PETHIDINE at the time.) He has CHOSEN his ruthless medical activities. He CHOOSES never to put out the trash. He CHOOSES to live in squalor in his attic eyrie with the toilet tipping over (he calls it the Leaning Tower of Pisser), he CHOOSES to live in a highly flammable maze of clothes, newspapers, patients' notes, videos and paint pots. He chose his EXISTENCE. He has ARRANGED for the stink that pervades, that precludes inviting anyone over. The place is UNINHABITABLE, and in it he broods on his ill-luck. His mother didn't like him much, his father was aloof. Yeah, yeah. But THIS is the man the neglected boy INVENTED, this is the guy he was willing at some point to BECOME: a sad-sack USER OF WOMEN.*

* Some of Dr Lewis's female patients joined a SUPPORT GROUP for victims of medical shenanigans. Every month, they got together for dreary meetings in which pain and anger were addressed, followed by lunch. In the afternoon, they worked on developing a POSITIVE ATTITUDE to their misfortunes.

So Dr Lewis didn't just mess up their BODIES. He'd made it necessary for them to go to these AWFUL MEETINGS.

THE GORGEOUS GORGE

Torn asunder when the world began, the rock and the lake remained estranged. The rock rested, an enormous CUBE, its perpendicular cliffs tricky for seals. A prison briefly stood there; earlier, a monastery; now an unmanned lighthouse only. The rest of it a yellow-white PRONG, schlong, dong, the colour of the necks of the gannets that gathered there.

The LAKE was left to ROT. People threw their DUNG in there, fish heads, bags of kittens, the carcasses of farm animals. They threw HUMAN BEINGS in too if they felt like it: witches, malefactors, stillborn babies, the OBESE. They all sank slowly to the bottom, arms outstretched, until the pond became a pestilential pool of slops and slime and DEATH GOO, the haunt of murderers, smugglers and suicides. Even the EELS died (and eels LOVE trash!).

So they DRAINED it. People are always draining things! Not just WOUNDS, or PASTA, but innocent things like MARSHLAND. Moisture incurs censure. It can never simply be LEFT. Baffled by an unseemly gulch of shame in the midst of their rural backwater, the locals decided to OBLITERATE it. But the lake didn't MEAN to be a slime-pool, it had slime forced UPON it! Ignored for a million years it might have recovered, CLEANSED itself, become a place for eels and ornamental swans again. But the locals couldn't wait: locals are so IMPATIENT.

At night, when her solitude is assured (and inescapable), this ancient, atrophied and misunderstood VOID heats up! Steam rises from her cracks and along her lonesome, loathsome paths. The gorge is ALIVE. She has lived SO LONG – and she longs, LONGS, for the rock. She plots – what? Reunion or retribution. And as she plots, her PLANES shift a bit. Trees sway, pebbles roll, flowers get temporarily buried, rabbit tunnels blocked. FORMIDABLE, as all cunts are, averse to abandonment or annihilation, she shudders ominously under her blanket of dust.

Through her dark and desiccated folds glides a gargantuan form: JEN. Sleepless, she paces. Like a blind emboldened RACEHORSE she pounds. Like a racehorse she stamps, kicking against her fate as she circles and re-circles her gorge. Jen can think of NOTHING now but ROGER LEWIS, his cleft chin, grey eyes and air of injury. She yearns for him, yowls, she YODELS for him! She seeks her own RUIN in Roger.

He is one of her SIX BLESSINGS! Jen has been reading too many *Take a Break* magazines, stolen from the waiting room. In the last issue, they advised their readers (some of the most flummoxed and forlorn folk around) to COUNT THEIR BLESSINGS: they were supposed to think up at least six blessings and then – COUNT them. It hasn't been easy for Jen to come up with so many, but she finally managed the following:

1. Her FOREHEAD. Jen's glad she has a forehead: she likes splashing WATER on it.
2. The jacuzzi. (A lot of forehead-splashing can be conducted there.)
3. Cargo pants. (DUNGAREES really.)
4. The TOMATO. Brought over from South America at some point and adapted by the Italians, the tomato has formed the basis of many a hearty meal for Jen.

5. Urma Thurb, although Jen hasn't FORGIVEN her yet (and never expects to see her again).
6. ROGER, his swivel hips spiralling in his swivel chair.

But tonight Jen only gets as far as the TOMATO before her blessings are substantially REDUCED by a faraway YELP coming from the surgery! She looks up at the dark building. Clouds are forming strangely above it. Lights flicker in the attic windows. There's another yelp, which sounds just like the laughing Jen heard when she was on the widow's walk. And those aren't CLOUDS moving above the house, but SMOKE, pouring from one of the windows.

THE SURGERY'S ON FIRE!!!

Jen charges uphill through the undergrowth, though RUNNING and going UPHILL are her least favourite modes of travel (no racehorse SHE!). But Jen is full of ZEAL to save Roger! It doesn't occur to her to phone the fire brigade when she reaches the house. She doesn't hesitate, she just starts clambering up the stairs. She might not MAKE it, she's so out of breath, but the occasion calls for HEROISM, self-sacrifice, it calls for a GLADIATOR, and that gladiator is JEN.

The door to his flat is slightly ajar, so she barges in. This is the first time Jen has ever seen his place, but there's no time now to dwell on the cherished objects of Roger's existence (she can't see them through the drifting smoke anyway). DUTY CALLS. Jen presses blindly on, panting, choking, calling, until she reaches the heart of the conflagration: Roger's bedroom. Jen is so intent on her mission she doesn't notice a tall figure sweeping past her as she enters the room, though she does hear a faint GIGGLE coming from somewhere. All Jen can see is ROGER, lying as Jen has always HOPED to see him: asleep in his bed.

But the bed is surrounded by FLAMES! Jen stumbles back down the hallway in search of the bathroom, throwing open every door in a PANIC until she finds it. She douses some towels in water and rushes back to SAVE WOGER! When she reaches him, she throws all the towels on top of him, then uses his duvet and pillows to smother the flames around the bed.

Waking to find Jen in his room, Roger for some reason thinks she's about to KILL him! He begs her not to kill THE CHILDREN. Jen is surprised. She's never even THOUGHT of killing Roger's children, Jen doesn't think about Roger's children from one week to the NEXT (unless they happen to invade the surgery, from which they are quickly expelled by Francine). On the other hand, she hasn't considered SAVING them either. So Jen sets off to FIND the stupid kids and make sure they're alive. She soon spots them in a doorway, rubbing their eyes. When they see HER, running at them, they quickly retreat into their room. Far from the aura of racehorse, there is more of the RHINOCEROS about Jen, in the heat of battle.

She returns to Roger to assure him that the kids are OK. As she enters his room, Roger LUNGES at her! In the haze of smoke he hasn't RECOGNISED her and has apparently mistaken Jen again for the ARSONIST. But when he realises it's her, he apologises and seems to relax. He starts pouring water over some clothes that are still smouldering in a corner. He is wearing, Jen notes, a day-glo green nylon dressing gown that will HAVE TO GO.

This seems as good a moment as any to shriek, 'WHAT HAPPENED?' – they both shriek it at the same time! Then Jen asks if she should call the fire brigade, but Roger is against the idea, claiming that everything's pretty much under control. Jen looks around the room, which looks like HELL: a HELL-HOLE.

'Who *did* this?' she asks him.

'Oh, these things happen. A bit of a firetrap, I'm afraid.'

Jen can't deny it, as she surveys the mountains of clothes

and papers and YOGHURT TUBS. She has always associated Roger with ORDER and WHITENESS, his white coat, his white paint, but now sees that Roger too is human. It charms her.

'Well, I guess I'll be off then,' she says. 'Downstairs. Back to the basement. If you don't NEED me any more, that is.'

At this, Roger crosses the room and clasps Jen to him! Jen turns PURPLE all over but hopes he can't see this in the gloom. Taking a gamble, she raises her face in anticipation of a KISS. But Roger is not in a kissing mood! He has just been almost SET ON FIRE and it has unnerved him. He leaps adroitly away to check on some more smouldering stuff.

Jen is HURT. What a let-down after all her exertions, the exertions of a RHINOCEROS, to be so dully dismissed. Down in the dungeon she cooks herself a HERO'S BREAKFAST and wonders who DID it, who set fire to Woger's bedroom? And who does all this SQUAWKING? Who has it in for WOGER? Could it be those weedy children who ask permission to BREATHE? Must be some bloody patient. Patients are the WORST.

ROGER & OUT

The need, late in life, to go suck on some TEAT, to be NURSED. Most turn to drink; Roger joined the Air Ambulance Service! Helicopters offered the best view he was ever going to get of geological excrescences that resemble breasts. Dr Lewis's ONLY interest in landscape was in its resemblance to breasts. There were many local hummocks, paps, bluffs and promontories he had long lusted to sink his teeth into.

He also craved EXCITEMENT, rescue missions, bad accidents on the highway, pain, death, gore, and looking DOWN on people. He had TIRED of his white doctor's garb – he coveted the ORANGE FLIGHT SUIT. It showed off his trim waist and hips! Even his CHIN CLEFT was becomingly lit by orange reflections bouncing off the suit. The straps under the crotch formed a protective LEDGE for his balls, which he found quite comfortable (unaware that the same straps, round the back, made his ass look like a VULVA). And he liked the LINGO. In the Air Ambulance Service you don't just say, 'Let's go over there.' You say: 'TWO MILES AT TWELVE O'CLOCK' (straight ahead), or 'FIVE MILES AT THREE O'CLOCK' (an abrupt turn to the right). There were all kinds of ALERTS too. Yellow, Green, Red – Roger had always wanted Alerts.

He returned from his heroic escapades ready to face with equanimity another boring afternoon of his own patients. And the flight suit had the desired effect: he became even more beloved in the community! PHOTOS of the dishy doc began to appear in the local paper, along with brief descriptions of his best emergencies. For one of these photos, they made Dr Lewis come into a STUDIO, where they attached a rope to the straps on his flight suit and hung him in the air! He was supposed to look MID-RESCUE, like Superman.

Soon he was being stalked by a pushy but appealing LADY REPORTER who wanted to write an IN-DEPTH PROFILE. She asked him a lot of technical questions, which Dr Lewis answered in his usual thorough manner, bombarding her with more info on helicopters and flight paths and Alerts than she'd ever dreamt! In his excitement he made the mistake of mentioning the Golden Hour, the crucial period within which seriously injured people are supposed to receive medical attention (he immediately regretted this, since he and Charlie, the pilot, RARELY managed to get to anybody within an hour). Whenever he SHUT UP, they would sit for a moment of mutual perplexity, then the lady reporter would snuggle up and they'd have a SNOG.

'Isn't she too FAT to be a nurse?' the lady reporter asked Roger one day after encountering Jen in the corridor (eighty-four). 'Looks too fat to me!'

'Good little worker though,' Roger offered in Jen's defence.

Jen HEARD this! How she ACHED for him – her EARS ached from being pressed so often against their adjoining wall. She too wanted to finger the plastic placket of his orange SCRUB SHIRT! She didn't like him talking about her behind her back to that skinny REPORTER BITCH. Surely men will TIRE one day of skinny women, once they realise how much VOMITING'S involved.

Down in the dungeon, a pretty, perky, skinny little party bag was put through untold miseries, the LEAST of which was having tomato soup injected into it until it BURST (ah, the tomato). But Jen saved the woman's article (HIGH-FLYING HERO SWOOPS AGAIN), and treasured the picture of Roger in his flight suit, hanging in the air.

He was busier than ever these days, and correspondingly ALOOF. He was too grand even to speak to Jen! He would push past her in the corridor (ninety-nine) mumbling, 'I'm sending you a collar bone and a sore throat. There's also a hand for later.' The guy no longer had time to mention WHOLE PATIENTS: he was narrowing things down to their essence.

When not airborne, Roger was on the phone to the General Medical Council, or writing them LETTERS, which Jen instantly had to post because, according to Roger's new lingo, they contained 'time-sensitive material' (they were late). His current dispute was with JEREMY, a patient who had thought he was DYING (because Dr Lewis had TOLD him he was). In view of his imminent demise, Jeremy had of course SOLD EVERYTHING and gone round the world. (Why do people DO this? But they do.)

When Jeremy got back from his travels, bewilderdly blooming with health, Dr Lewis informed him that he was not dying after all, there had just been a bit of a MIX-UP with the files. (ANOTHER guy had meanwhile died, with no warning whatsoever from Dr Lewis.) You'd think Jeremy would have been PLEASED to find out he wasn't dying but he was FURIOUS. For, though somewhat better acquainted with GEOGRAPHY, Jeremy was now FLAT BROKE. Dr Lewis had to explain to the General Medical Council that it was an HONEST MISTAKE that anyone who'd mixed Jeremy's file up with somebody else's could have made and he would have told Jeremy sooner if he could have FOUND him, but Jeremy was in VENEZUELA or TIBET by then and therefore unreachable. Doctors can't be expected to keep track of everyone all the time.

The only patient Dr Lewis looked forward to these days

was Martha, the ORGASMIC WOMAN, whose doses of electricity, Seroxat and Valium went on without any sign of improvement so far (if having fewer orgasms can be called an improvement). Instead, Martha seemed to get a big KICK out of every experimental treatment Dr Lewis could think up, her appreciation audible through the walls of the consulting room. Jen had already tried to EAT the handbag she'd assigned to Martha, an ugly brown WOOL affair with leather handles like BINGO WINGS and CROCHETED decorative elements, after stuffing it with PARMA HAM: it was a ham-bag sandwich! She had chewed and chewed it, and had made some progress with the RIM and the icky woollen clasp, but wasn't getting anywhere with the HANDLES, and the whole thing was beginning to ALARM her, since the dye stained her cheeks and she didn't know how long Parma ham LASTS.

Roger was so busy and self-important now that he was too busy to have a GIRLFRIEND. He found the lady reporter's incessant questions exhausting and, when she started asking for FREE MEDICAL ADVICE, he knew it was over. So he DUMPED her. But JEN didn't know this. JEN had reached a peak, a pitch, a PAP, of jealousy. WHAT AM I, A ROBOT, AN AUTOMATON, a nurse MACHINE? Does he think that, just because I am poor, obscure, ugly, huge and weird, I have no FEELINGS? When he PRICKS me, do I not bleed?! Does he think I can just carry on mopping brows and living in the basement, and mean NOTHING to him?

In fury she slipped out of the surgery one day and went to see the Eakinses. Jen had been put in charge of May ever since her return home after her stroke. Jen was supposed to go over there and check May's BLOOD PRESSURE every now and then. There wasn't much else they could do for May. She could barely walk (the physiotherapists had given up on her) or talk (ditto, the SPEECH therapists). She couldn't read or write or concentrate well enough to be read TO. She couldn't even watch TV, except maybe GOLF programmes. It wasn't clear how much she understood. May was a mass of DEFICITS, deficiencies – but she was HAPPY. She sang, she smoked, she drank wine! And she kissed everybody's hand when they came to see her.

She kissed JEN's hand now, and offered to share her lipstick with her – May touched up her own lipstick frequently throughout the day. She LOVED lipstick! Since the stroke, May's former disapproval of everything had dissolved into APPROVAL: everything was now OK WITH MAY. Marvin felt the same! People (old friends and colleagues) were always telling him to put May in a NURSING HOME, or just let her DIE of one of her many bronchial problems – but he didn't WANT to. That would mean the marriage was over, and he didn't want it to end.

He went off now to make Jen her EIGHTEENTH nice hot cup of tea of the day. But Jen hadn't come for TEA. Nor did she appreciate May's insistent offering of lipstick (make-up being a sore point with Jen). She was OFFENDED by May's contentment and affability, her warm spot by the fire, her loyal hubby. Jen was convinced that Dr Lewis was applying DEEP-TISSUE MASSAGE at that very moment to either Martha or the reporter bitch, maybe BOTH, and she could stand no more.

It cannot be stated too emphatically how DANGEROUS self-hatred is. IT IS RESPONSIBLE FOR ALL TRAGEDY. It will bring the whole species to its KNEES. Hitler, Oscar Wilde, Elvis, Caligula, Walt Disney, the Hutus, Nixon, Oppenheimer – they all hated themselves. It's a BIG PROBLEM.

Jen scrabbled around in her bottomless bag for a syringe and quietly injected May with some spare INSULIN she just happened to have left over from some other poor slob. Then she smothered May with one of her comfy cushions. By the time Marvin arrived with the tea, May was unconscious! Jen, playing the Heroine of the Hour, called Dr Lewis, who rushed over, his defibrillator dragging romantically on the ground behind him.

Roger did all he could until Charlie could get there and whisk May off in the helicopter – Marvin had to make his own way to the hospital, on LAND (they never had room for RELATIVES in that thing!).

From the hospital, May was eventually sent to a nursing home, from which she never escaped! Marvin visited her there every day, but she wasn't allowed cigarettes or wine any more, nor did she get to see much golf on the communal telly. May was left slouched in a chair all day, eating MICRO-WAVED PUDDINGS that burnt her tongue. At night, nurses lifted her up off the loo by her BREASTS and yelled at her for soiling the bed.

But JEN was pleased by her little adventure. She liked the way Roger's lips thinned when he DEFIBRILLATED. She had always liked to see the doctors on the Children's Ward confused and sweaty, as they tried to revive some kid who'd turned navy-blue. Jen had turned navy-blue herself, from the EXCITEMENT of it all, whenever she called the Crash Team. Of course it wasn't NICE of her to inject sick kids with insulin and vincristine. But we're told EVERY DAY that there are too many PEOPLE in the world! We can't AFFORD to be sentimental about human life any more.

We're ALL mass murderers anyway: we live with the ATOM BOMB. Our names should REFLECT this better. No more Jills, Jeremys, Jeans and Jeanettes. We should all be called ZIT, ZILCH, ZERO. We should all be called LOATHE SELF.

SHARP MOMENTS

Though he'd joined the Air Ambulance Service for the sake of geological titillation, Dr Lewis's study of landscape soon palled. You lose DETAIL, the further you get from the earth. Instead of mountainous MAJUNGAS, he found he was preoccupied by CHARLIE and the other paramedics, their romantic ups and downs, who had the best CAR, music system, and sporting highlights RECALL, as well as head winds, wind speed and cold fronts. Only PATIENTS now relieved the ennui!

One day, Dr Lewis had four emergencies in a row! The first was a student who'd been stabbed outside a pub and had lain near by all night, semiconscious. Dr Lewis decided the stab wound was only superficial and gave the guy some dyspepsia medicine. (He died five days later – that wasn't DYSPEPSIA, that was peritonitis!)

Next, they went to the aid of a drunk old geezer who'd got himself run over by a truck. He was too drunk to tell Dr Lewis what was wrong with him, so Dr Lewis told him to go sleep it off and see his own GP in the morning. (But the poor fellow had EIGHTEEN BROKEN RIBS and died in the night!)

NEXT, they landed in the middle of a yellow field of RAPE (and really SPOILT it) to see a woman in a secluded caravan. A distraught man bustled them inside, and there on the floor lay VIRGINIA, the American with the HRT scruples! This was the first time Dr Lewis had come upon one of his own patients during his Air Ambulance work, and it was quite a surprise. The husband told him Virginia had woken up that morning unable to MOVE. Her left arm and left leg both seemed to be paralysed. Also, she'd been vomiting for hours and her speech was slurred (so nobody knew that what she was trying to say right now was: 'Get that mother-fucking asshole outta here!').

Virginia had had some kind of SEIZURE (brought on by HRT), but Dr Lewis liked to leave no stone unturned – especially when wearing his flight suit. He slowly tapped his dimpled chin, and combed his fingers through his hair, that stood like a field of RAPE on top of his head, while he ticked off the various diagnostic possibilities. The vomiting could be caused by food poisoning, gastroenteritis, Ménière's disease, roundworm infection, migraine, Addison's disease, acute labyrinthitis, diabetes, kidney trouble, hepatitis, or cancer. The general weakness on her left side: pernicious anaemia, an underactive thyroid or adrenal gland, heart failure, poliomyelitis, polymyositis, rheumatoid arthritis, diabetes, systemic lupus erythematosus, a transient ischaemic attack, neuritis, motor neurone disease, or cancer.

Charlie was revving the helicopter blades impatiently outside. It was time for ACTION. Dr Lewis decided it must be cancer, having suddenly remembered the lump he'd found in her breast (she had already had the mastectomy he predicted she would need – though, as it turned out, the lump was BENIGN). So he gave her some penicillin and steroids, told her to go back to the oncologist, and left her LYING ON THE FLOOR.

Was it a BIRD, was it a PLANE? No, a doctor.

Next, they had to escort the corpse of a six-year-old girl to hospital to await the arrival of her mother. The kid had been playing on the pavement outside her childminder's house when a car knocked her down. She had died instantly, but the mother couldn't be told that over the phone, so Dr Lewis had to WAIT. And WAIT! By the time the frantic mother finally made her way to the hospital, Dr Lewis had had THREE CUPS OF TEA. So, naturally, he was in the LOO. When he got out, he duly explained to the woman that her daughter was dead. She became hysterical! Dr Lewis *told* her death is part of life, but she wouldn't LISTEN. You share these findings with people, discoveries made over the course of DECADES of medical practice, and they pay no attention!

Jen was waiting for him in the field behind the surgery (he had rigged up a rudimentary LANDING PAD for himself there). He'd just rung the surgery from the helicopter to tell her he would be landing in approximately four minutes thirty seconds and sure enough, down he fluttered! As Charlie sped off to Air Ambulance HQ, Jen found herself alone in the dusk with Roger. The sight of him in his orange flight suit, luminous as a slab of WIENER SCHNITZEL, was heart-rending. Though she was just supposed to be helping him CARRY stuff, Jen felt an urgent need to be FREE and unrestricted by DUTY.

Twisting her little upside-down nursy watch from its accustomed place on her mountainous nursy bosom, she tried to wrestle Roger to the ground! He was dumbfounded. He had always planned to acknowledge his gratitude some day for the way she'd saved his life in the fire, a token of appreciation, a BRACELET perhaps, or a new swivel chair. But as she tore wildly at his flight suit, Roger suddenly recalled how much he liked the SIZE of her: AMPLE GIRL. Jen was made for better things than just spreading Vaseline on old folks' KNEES!

He tried to get his arms around her but COULDN'T. So instead he fled with her back to the surgery, her white nursy hat bouncing on her head. Down the stairs they hurried, ass over heel, and arsy-versy, to Jen's bedroom, where Roger tied her to the bed. Then he attached himself by the straps of his flight suit to a pulley on the ceiling that Jen had never noticed before. He had astonishing CONTROL of this device: he could raise and lower himself over Jen with great rapidity, and a certain rigidity, keeping up a steady rhythm. Jen became the rudimentary LANDING PAD for his touch-downs! Pinioned and helpless, she stared up at his orange-tinted face as he bungee-jumped all over her, wanting only to envelop him further.

To achieve greater accuracy, he grabbed her breasts. These were usually immune to all sensation, but Dr Lewis's antics resulted in hitherto unknown twinges in Jen's viscerals. He rose and fell like a COLOSSUS over the desert that was Jen, journeying over her land masses, copping a feel of her pyramids. Her PARAMETERS were less definable: Jen had always felt like an AMORPHOUS BLOB (and she WAS one).

There were SHARP MOMENTS in all this for Jen. Sometimes Dr Lewis's cleft CHIN, with its five o'clock shadow, grazed her cheek (TWO CENTIMETRES AT FIVE O'CLOCK), or her undergarments snagged on some bit of plastic on his orange-wrapped thighs. But these were only INKLINGS of the torments to come.

A SHAKY AFFAIR

Thus Dr Lewis and Jen embarked on a shaky affair! These doctor–nurse things are always complicated because your lovemaking can so easily be interrupted by PATIENTS and their frequent need to DIE or have BABIES or a STROKE. Always there is duty.

And yet, anyone peeking through the surgery windows early in the morning might have caught a glimpse of Dr Lewis lying NAKED on a trolley, with a sheet draped across his middle and his legs wide open. But those weren't Dr Lewis's legs, they were JEN'S! She would be under the sheet with Dr Lewis's COCK down her throat, while the trolley slowly rolled them across the floor.

During quiet periods during the working day, they would take their steaming hot cups of tea or coffee downstairs and play: DOCTORS & NURSES! He would poke her with all the instruments in his medical bag; she would take his penis's blood pressure, using her special tight-fitting children's cuff, or give him rectal examinations that swept him off his feet. Sometimes he CATHETERISED her and filled her bladder with SALINE solution (?) – they made use of all kinds of equipment in their amorosities. They injected each other with uppers, downers, amyl nitrite and all the other aphrodisiacs mentioned in footnotes in the *BMJ*. He rubbed that ASS of hers until the building shook! (Francine had to realign the pictures of water mills in the waiting room – she thought there must be volcanic activity in the area.)

When his bollocking of her backside got the better of him, Dr Lewis would tie Jen to the bed and LEAVE her, while he saw a few patients! As soon as he got a chance, he'd rush down, SAW OFF Jen's clothing with a scalpel, squeeze her breasts, and rush OUT again, tucking his erection away as he ran! TWENTY MINUTES might elapse before he dashed back and FUCKED her, coming almost immediately from the excitement of DELAY. Had he known how unerotic all this was for JEN – well, he still would have done it.

SHARP MOMENTS. It isn't always easy being involved with a DOCTOR, a doctor consumed by DUTY. His aloofness still troubled her, as did the FOOTBALL. He still hadn't RECOGNISED her either – perhaps he never would! He also liked visiting a nearby MOTOR MUSEUM a lot, housed in an old army hangar. It was FREEZING in there! He and Jen were usually the only visitors, breathing steam all over the classic cars, or the antique petrol cans and tin ads for oil and tyres. Jen put up with a LOT in that hangar.

She understood of course that Roger couldn't be with her ALWAYS. He was crucial to the community. And then there were his KIDS. Jen couldn't tell if Edward and Adele were particularly fine examples or not, but she resented them. Because of those mangy kids, Jen was never allowed to visit Roger upstairs. He wanted to keep their affair SACRED and SECRET for a while. Jen had many SEPARATIONS to endure.

Yet Roger had true feelings for Jen. He had noticed, for instance, that Jen's ass, stiffened, could be wrapped in a PUDDING CLOTH and set on fire! Doused with brandy, her ass took on an ELEMENTAL air, making it seem patriotic and festive!

But it was her collection of HANDBAGS that really stirred him. It was like a HAREM in there! Dr Lewis had previously been IMMUNE to handbags, quelled, even a little REPELLED by them. They were WOMEN'S stuff: degenerate and dirty. Of course he'd noticed that some were more LIKEABLE than others, some softer, some sturdy, some so BULKY there was no adequate division between the world inside the bag and the world OUTSIDE. But he had always been perturbed by their inviolability and alienness, their dubious function and contents, hiding secret things like money and love letters and items designed for soaking LIQUIDS up. You never really know WHAT'S in a handbag.

But now, staring up at the handbags amid the stink of Jen's pussy, as she lay like a DEAD FISH beside him in the bed (trying, through total IMMOBILITY, to keep her flab from flopping), Roger became entranced by the variety of colour and shape that is available in the handbag universe. Each bag seemed to have a different PERSONALITY. It was like having a big bunch of front and back BOTTOMS pinned to the wall, awaiting his every whim!

He was fascinated by their presence in the BUILDING, and seduced by their insistent call! While Jen was out on her rounds (changing bandages, taking blood pressure, emptying bedpans, administering laxatives and enemas, weighing babies, kicking cats: her Health Visits), Dr Lewis was drawn to the basement to handle those HANDBAGS, to fondle and molest them, burying his face in them, sometimes his whole head! He became quite a CONNOISSEUR.

After a bout of these clandestine intimacies, he would retreat upstairs and swivel in his swivel chair, dreaming of being a great diagnostician like Dr Kildare, or a neurosurgeon like Ben Casey. His RIGHT to be one or the other! He was certainly HANDSOME enough.

THE VEIL

It was a perfect match!! They were happy only when together – and they were hardly ever apart! There was no END to their caresses, nor to the tenderness they felt for each other. Utter acceptance, utter devotion, utter need, utter hope. FOR EVER. The life-giving warmth of two bodies touching, the softness of skin against skin, of breath and murmuring.

It was a symbiosis that really WORKED, for Jen at least. She became accustomed to the constant contact, protection, sympathy and love. Their connection was Jen's LIFE BLOOD, the biggest and best thing in the world! Such passion *must* be MUTUAL, no? No.

Held in her mother's strong grasp, against her mother's warm chest, it never occurred to Jen that the same big arms could be used for SHOVING or ABANDONING. But then there came the fateful day when Jen's mother decided, OUT OF THE BLUE, that it was time for Jen to learn to have a regular afternoon nap. A nap, scheduled and timed! Jen didn't want or need this nap, she just wanted to be with her MOTHER, but her mother put her in her cot and left her there! Jen cried and cried in her sky-blue bedroom, receiving no reply, no consolation, not even an instant COOKIE. She was just some sort of PARCEL that could be put down and FORGOTTEN about! She was NOTHING to her mother. Jen sat looking through the bars of her cot at the door to her room, then up at the blank blue walls, and cried until she conked out (and had her nap after all). She woke to face another stint in the world, but a world that had *changed*, turned on her, turned sour. A world full of BETRAYAL.

Birds are making a lot of noise as Jen trudges through the gorge, but she doesn't notice them (we are a poor audience for birds). After her Health Visits, nursing here, nursing there, Jen skives in the gorge. Roger won't mind. Busy man. Jen is trying to LIKE herself, for Roger's sake: she's RUSHING the process a little in fact! *Take a Break* says no one can like you unless you like yourself. This seems most UNJUST, and EXTREMELY inconvenient for JEN. She's got to try to like herself QUICK, before Roger REALISES she DOESN'T like herself and, as a result, goes OFF her!

But it ain't EASY, with her puckered, pockmarked breasts, her monotonous voice, her tangled thicket of hair and fungal irregularities and rickety knees and all those CATS she's kicked. Jen has worn herself OUT with the two main difficulties in life: disliking oneself and being disliked by others. She's now pretty much BEYOND heartbreak: she can only PECK at love. She circles and re-circles her ROGER, poking about for his regurgitated CRUMBS.

Jen sits down on a mossy bank. The grass around her is covered with tiny blue, yellow and white flowers, and iridescent dew. Flies flit about, all trying to sit on the same warm sunny white leaf: it's like MUSICAL CHAIRS down there! But Jen doesn't notice. Nature is LOST on Jen. There's a VEIL between Jen and the outside world that stops her SEEING things, a veil of BETRAYAL. Pink horse chestnut trees and dark-blue hills hover over her IN VAIN. They mean NOTHING to her. Jen is like some giant CYCLOPS, one-eyed and numb, a crushed, crouched creature hiding in a corner of her own LIFE. Even her NAME is crushed, a small crumpled HANKY of a name, strangely curtailed. She feels

DISINHERITED: the world doesn't BELONG to her, nor she to it. The world never seems real to Jen unless she's EATING a bit of it.

An ANIMAL takes on its environment, considers it real and worthy of investigation! Jen sees her environment as something that needs to be DEFEATED. What does JEN have in common with a bird singing its heart out in a chosen tree? Nothing.

Animals aren't pussy-footing around about life, feeling VAGUE about stuff, waiting for something to HAPPEN. It's already happening, and it's IMPORTANT. For bugs, for birds, life is for real, EVERY TIME! Jen has SUSPENDED her life somewhere, coldly cast it aside. She has CRUSHED love, companionship, crushed everything in her path with ANGER. She has bandaged every HURT with anger, filled her every waking moment with it.

She has perfected the art of being UNREACHABLE: people treat her like she's in a WHEELCHAIR, and she treats them the same way! She has HIDDEN herself in nursing, not just as a form of ATONEMENT but as an infinite resource, a bottomless pit, of ANGER (towards patients). She has tried to atone for her mother's death by never being happy, never being loved, never GIVING love, never being beautiful or successful or even competent, never being LIKED, never being part of the world.

ANIMALS aren't afraid of love. They love without shame, BRAVELY. Animals know everything they need to know. A sea urchin at three days old is everything it's going to be! A chiton at TWO days old. No one blames a CHITON for its mother's death. A chiton doesn't blame itself.

'Nice walk?' asks Roger when Jen wanders into the consulting room. 'How are they all, our noble patients?'

'Stable,' Jen replies. 'But they all seem to think they'd get better a lot faster if they went to Thailand or BELIZE and learnt to DIVE. Why does everybody have to go to BELIZE?'

This is a sore point, since Roger too wants to go to Belize! Roger is APPALLED by Jen's indifference to Belize.

'You old stick-in-the-mud!' he says, grabbing her ass and pulling her on to his lap. 'You'd better just stay here then, hadn't you, *forever.*'

Jen tries to imagine this 'forever'. She has forever expected to DIE, or be KILLED! She has forever expected to be deprived of what she WANTS. She has forever assumed herself to be an OUTCAST.

The swivel chair, under their combined weight, starts to roll across the floor at frightening speed. Roger puts out a foot to stop it, but too violently: they both fall off. Practically BURIED under her, Roger breathlessly cries out, 'Marry me!'

'Eh?'

But it's TRUE: Roger wants to marry Jen! It makes perfect sense to ROGER, for he can think of nothing worse than being parted from those HANDBAGS of hers. He's determined to make HONEST BAGS of them all!

A SUNNY SCENE

A sunny scene up to now, was it not? Handbags, helicopters, steady incomes, docile patients, well-fed bellies, sideburns cropped with care. GOOD-LOOKING PEOPLE going about their lawful business in an organised manner, everything running PRETTY DAMN SMOOTHLY.

But what if getting together is about the WORST THING this pair could do? What if it's bad for the WORLD? Doctor–nurse books never pause to consider whether romance is really such a GOOD thing. We're all so KEEN on it, so sure where we stand when two people of opposite sex, with leisure time and no apparent impediments, flop into bed. Millions of years, millions of matings, have encouraged us to find such conjunctions SWEET, harmless, moving, IMPORTANT. Poets have exhausted themselves crooning about it, novelists too (it's MUCH more exhausting writing a novel). We're trained from birth to CELEBRATE love, to sing, dance, drink, think and FUCK in its honour.

But what if it's NOT so nice? What if, given over-population and the nature of the species in general, human sexual love is actually pointless, evil, embarrassing, depressing and DOOMED? And what if the whole purpose of love affairs is not what it SEEMS, the intense, narcissistic and sentimental APPRECIATION of someone else – but instead, the usual end result: deciding the beloved STINKS? What if we're biologically programmed to UNDERVALUE each other? What if it's DISGUST, not love, that makes the world go round? Maybe evolution favours creatures that never get too happy, for that might make them wild and reckless, unreliable as reticules for GENES, which is all we are.

O the mind, mind has mountains; cliffs of fall
Frightful, sheer, no-man-fathomed. Hold them cheap
May who ne'er hung there.

Gerard Manley Hopkins

THE WEDDING PLANS

Can there be anything more preposterous than a lavish wedding? WHY must fornication be recognised in this way? Just DOING it should be reward enough!

The whole point of weddings is to INSULT everybody, the bride, the bride's father, the ushers, the flower girls, the organist, the guests, even MENDELSSOHN: weddings make everyone feel like CRAP. Brides by the score are driven DEMENTED organising these things! You see them hanging around street corners in HORNS and ANTENNAE, and T-shirts that say 'I'M A SLAG'. Even weddings that don't HAPPEN take their toll – you still have to CANCEL everything you ordered (cake, flowers, church, priest, priest-ess, guru, ORGANIST, bikini wax, honeymoon) before the traumatic decizh was made.

The TREES that have vanished to produce the wedding INVITES and RSVPs and THANK-YOU notes that brides and their mothers spend so many argumentative evenings designing, addressing, stamping and mailing! The MONEY, that would have come in so handy for the MARRIAGE, or the DIVORCE, that's poured instead into feeding a laconic horde CHICKEN ROULADE and MELON. The reunions – so needless! – of friend and foe. The RINGS and things. The carefully constructed CHARACTERLESSNESS of it all, the CONFORMISM. Why does it have to be so Mrs

BEETONISH? The show, the sham, the shame, and all for WHAT? So that the guests can buy cooking utensils at John Lewis and rent Edwardian outfits and dance Highland reels and devote AN ENTIRE DAY AND NIGHT to making sure two dopes get hitched? So the bride's father can hand her over to some poor schmuck to FUCK? How revolting. You hate a world in which such things HAPPEN. You hate YOURSELF. (You're supposed to.)

Dr Lewis wanted the WORKS. He wanted a church wedding and he wanted all his patients to come and he wanted his favourite hymns sung and sung LOUD. He interviewed three different live bands and hired TWO, the second as back-up in case the first one went quiet. He lined up a photographer who had a cheap deal going on fake-leather photo albums. He ordered a three-tiered wedding cake with circular pillars that looked like a Pompeiian villa primed to COLLAPSE under the weight of Dr Lewis's demands. He even persuaded Jen to get fitted for a wedding dress which, through complicated corsetry, was two-tiered and gave her a WAIST. The petticoats were manifold. She looked like a meringue.

Jen's only requirement was that the wedding should be SOON. She didn't think she could handle a long ENGAGEMENT, which (she assumed) would feel like an interminable DATE. Jen had never been on a date during which she didn't wish she was home eating ice cream instead (it always seemed such a PALAVER before the FUCKING could begin). She was already in a state of HIGH ALERT, convinced she would LOSE Roger at any moment! She was WRITHING with uncertainty about him. Either he would go off her because she was unable to LOVE HERSELF enough, or he'd be stolen by some envious creep in the neighbourhood. Jen regarded every other woman now with the deepest suspicion, even Francine. ESPECIALLY Francine!

Francine's behaviour since the announcement of their

INTENTIONS had been noticeably erratic. She was often absent from her post, the cups of TEA stopped coming, and she seemed to have embarked on a FRENZY of make-overs! What TV show was she WATCHING? Her hair kept changing colour, size and shape: sometimes angular, sometimes TRIANGULAR, sometimes cuboid, sometimes spiralling out of control! BOTOX too seemed to have a role in her transformations – there were days when Francine's forehead was so smooth she couldn't even look peeved with PATIENTS.

She was so CHAMELEONIC! Jen suspected that it was all a ploy to STEAL ROGER, once Francine managed to zero in on the right look. But why now? Why hadn't Francine made a pass YEARS AGO, if she was after him? Now it was JEN'S turn.

Jen's extreme state of engagement-anxiety was alleviated NOT by taking out wedding insurance, but by anaesthetising herself with WEDDING FOOD. The caterers kept sending samples of chicken roulade and devilled eggs to try. And there were a number of cheap champagnes also – Jen was somehow supposed to decide which was the best. So she burped, she barfed, she ballooned (putting the old wedding dress idea in jeopardy), and she blamed Roger daily for not HELPING more.

She had no one to invite. But in a drunken moment she defiantly mailed a few leftover invitations to both her brother and Urma Thurb. She expected no reply – but they were coming! Urma Thurb had even volunteered to be the matron of honour! After her years in the hospital, Urma Thurb was no longer touchy about the word 'MATRON' (she was alone in this).

Urma Thurb was PLEASED for Jen. She had never expected anything to go RIGHT for her. She had been worrying about the girl ever since their days on the Children's Ward together, when so many inexplicable EMERGEN-

CIES had erupted during Jen's shifts: monitors turned themselves off so that kids died without warning, the keys to the insulin fridge and drugs cabinet kept going missing, and the Crash Team was always being called to assist with BRAIN DEATHS or HEART ATTACKS, in children who'd only come in to have their TONSILS out!

Urma Thurb had of course been impressed by Jen's sang-froid, though Jen's indifference to her patients sometimes seemed a bit EXTREME, even in a NURSE. But who cares about a bunch of KIDS anyway? Plenty more where they came from, an endless supply in fact (as an exasperated Urma Thurb had often remarked to Jen when they faced yet another bed shortage).

Urma Thurb would be sorry to leave TONY behind (he couldn't accompany her to the wedding, he was in the middle of rewiring the Liver and Intestinal Diseases Department), and their THREE-IN-A-BED SEX SESSIONS, which he organised so well. Urma Thurb never had to TALK to the other girl – she would just arrive at the beginning and disappear before dawn. Tony was so good at CHOREOGRAPHING the thing too, humping one while licking the other, then ARSY-VERSY!

Afterwards, they would all lie in a ROW between each other's legs, like ROWERS, Urma Thurb usually at the BOTTOM, Tony sandwiched in between, and the girl at the HELM, smoking a cigarette. At such times Urma Thurb sometimes felt crushed, CRUSHED – but it was worth it.

THE WEDDING-EVE SUPPER

So, after reluctantly bidding farewell to her hard-working hubby, Urma Thurb took a train to Jen's rural backwater, and now sat mute in the back of Roger's Jag with Jen beside her. Jen's brother Nicky was in the front seat, admiring Roger's upholstery. They were all on their way to the WEDDING-EVE SUPPER at a local fish restaurant that was supposed to be good.

Unfortunately, they ordered PAELLA, which took FORTY-FIVE MINUTES to come and was NOT good. The rice was still hard, the whole thing was covered with pickled squid bits and KERNELS of salmon (?) dry as Grape Nuts, and it tasted OFF. They had ordered a pile of PAST-IT PAELLA! (But what do WEDDING GUESTS care about food? These are people willing to eat MELON-ON-STICKS with THREE HUNDRED GOOPS they don't know!)

The long wait for the paella gave Nicky a chance to exchange many a WISECRACK with Roger over medical matters – Nicky had always been a SUCKER for doctors. (They liked him too!) He also found time to mock, scold and GRILL Jen on everything from her paltry INCOME to her uselessness on the CLARINET.

As children, when not eating Grape Nuts (their father's favourite cereal), they had both been forced to play the clarinet, all because their father believed the clarinet's RE-

PERTOIRE was superior to any other instrument's. But Jen never got anywhere near the clarinet's REPERTOIRE: she could barely blow a note! She had MOUTH ULCERS the whole time, brought on by the REEDS or, psychosomatically, by her reluctance to PLAY. She thought she was going to ASPHYXIATE on that thing! Her clarinet misery only ended when her kind clarinet teacher told her father that Jen was too YOUNG to play the clarinet: she didn't have the LUNG CAPACITY. You have to be at least ELEVEN, he declared. (This didn't explain why NICKY had been playing the clarinet with APLOMB since the age of SIX.)

WHILE he grilled Jen, Nicky kept looking over her head to see who else was in the restaurant, CRANING his neck as if someone more interesting might come along any minute. Jen had forgotten what it was like to be with Nicky. Urma Thurb was no help – she was missing Tony and didn't say much. Roger was kept happy by all Nicky's flattery and seemed to think everything was going very well! But Jen was disappointed. It was months since she'd seen either of these people, and there seemed to be so little to SAY. She wasn't just angry, she was BORED.

After tasting the paella, Jen ordered a big bowl of CHIPS to have on the side, despite a disapproving glance from Nicky (still trying to STARVE her). Now he launched into her TEENAGE YEARS: fat as a house, draped in sacklike clothing, eating Grape Nuts and smoking dope in the middle of the day behind closed curtains, and failing her O levels. But isn't that what MOST people's teenage years are like? The real mistake was in letting Nicky pay for the wedding-eve supper – he seemed to think it entitled him to disclose every mortifying detail of Jen's past he could remember. Next he'd be telling them how Jen's NIGHTIE rose up once when they were small and Nicky saw her TINKLER and LAUGHED AND LAUGHED. Jen decided to pre-empt this by asking Nicky where her half of the dough was on the FLAT SALE.

'The flat sale, huh?! There wouldn't have BEEN a sale if I'd left it up to you!' cried Nicky. 'You and your TUBA BAND.' And Nicky went on to tell Roger and Urma Thurb all about Jen's attempt to sabotage the transaction, until he was almost hysterical with glee! DRUNK, Jen thought. She wanted to SLAP him. (With a tuba.)

Then Nicky almost denied them all DESSERT! He'd forgotten all ABOUT dessert! He was about to get the BILL before they'd HAD any! When Jen pointed this out, he relented and graciously asked Jen, as the MATRIARCH OF THE FAMILY, what she wanted for dessert. She said ICE CREAM. Nicky ordered one piece of CHEESECAKE for them all to share! How rude. Nicky KNEW Jen hated cheesecake. Just because Nicky was paying, and NICKY liked cheesecake, didn't mean they ALL had to eat cheesecake, or watch NICKY eating cheesecake, at the WEDDING-EVE SUPPER.

Jen went to the loo and SEETHED. She didn't care if Nicky used this as an opportunity to talk about her *behind her back*, or even as an opportunity to SNOG ROGER, as he'd clearly wanted to do all evening. Jen just wanted to be ALONE. Fuck the wedding, the presents, the JOB, the fiancé, Urma Thurb's discomfort. Fuck ICE CREAM.

She hadn't been sleeping well. There had been weird scufflings in the night, and more of that silly SQUAWKING. It filled Jen with foreboding. Maybe this whole wedding thing was a SET-UP for the biggest humiliation of her life: absent groom, sneering guests, Mendelssohn delays and whalebone insurrection?

There was nothing to look at in the loo except the usual anti-menstruation sign. Why is there a warning in every public toilet forbidding the disposal of menstrual products down the loo? SURE, shit, vomit, drugs, condoms, stillborn babies, secret documents, weapons of mass destruction, even whole plates of SPAGHETTI are FINE, but a TAMPON, or just the WRAPPER off a tampon? NO. For that you need a serious-looking MEDICAL BAG and an INCINERATOR – as if menstruation's some kind of communicable DISEASE. They've had HUNDREDS OF YEARS to come up with a toilet capable of handling this stuff but there's no will to do it! Much more fun to watch women squirm with guilt and shame. The cunt requires CONSTANT APOLOGY.

No ropes or blindfolds that night! After dropping Nicky and Urma Thurb off at their B & B, Roger went straight upstairs in demure recognition of the wedding eve. Jen thought of having a dip in the JACUZZI but there was a dark RING around it that she hadn't left there herself. Somebody else must have been in her flat that evening, enjoying JEN'S JACUZZI! So she gave it a miss and went to bed. She dreamt that she and Urma Thurb ate so many meringues they EXPLODED, which was a great relief.

Jen was woken by squawking outside, and the sound of Roger attempting to quieten somebody. Her fiancé was IN PERIL. Jen leapt out of bed, rushed up the basement steps, and threw open the front door. She could see Roger struggling in the car-park with some WOMAN.

'What's happening, Roger?' Jen called out from the front step.

Roger and the woman froze. 'Don't worry, darling,' he called back. 'Go to bed.'

'But don't you need some help?' asked Jen.

'No, I can handle it, thanks.'

So Jen went back to bed, wondering if the woman outside was the one who had squawked so often from some secret realm of the house and scrabbled in the gravel outside her windows night after night and maybe even used her JACUZZI. To sum up, had that duck been paddling in her pond?

THE WEDDING ITSELF

Urma Thurb arrived first thing to help Jen into her wedding dress. It had been hanging for three days on the door of Jen's office, so Jen was a little worried that it might smell of blood, guts and FORMALDEHYDE, but as soon as they opened the door they realised things were even worse: there were swathes of white satin and TULLE all over the floor! It looked like it had SNOWED in there.

Jen snatched the dress off the hook and examined it under the desk lamp. The OUTER layers were fine; but inside, the many petticoats had been viciously, violently, angrily TORN and shredded, not just the cotton and satin flounces but the really stiff icky ITCHY whorls of tulle netting that were supposed to make the dress stick out even more than it naturally WOULD with JEN in it. It's a pity we ever became tulle-users.

'What is going on here?' asked Urma Thurb in a tone Jen knew well from the old days: it was the tone Urma Thurb had used when Jen forgot to bring her WHISKY.

'How do *I* know?' Jen said defensively. 'It was OK yesterday!' Dangling in the bodice were a pair of sewing scissors given to her a few days before by a patient who couldn't make it to the wedding (too SICK). Or NAIL scissors. Jen hadn't been too sure WHAT kind of scissors they were (what did Jen know about SEWING?). Now she knew they were *wedding-shredding scissors*! Only an hour to go and the dress was a MESS!

There was no time to DWELL on such matters however. It was still wearable, if less puffy than planned, and it was Jen's duty to put it on. She struggled into the thing from below, like a POTHOLER. When she reached AIR and LIGHT again, Urma Thurb laced her up, creating that surprising WAIST. Then Jen clambered up on to her swivel chair and let Urma Thurb TWIRL her in order to affix a red cummerbund to Jen's MIDRIFF, making Jen look like TWO meringues, with JAM squidging out in between. The cummerbund was a souvenir of URMA THURB'S wedding: a piece of the red carpet she and Tony had walked along.

NICKY turned up in the middle of this operation. It sent him into a fit of GIGGLES. He called her 'the meringue of the family'! Dizzy from the twirling, Jen hardly knew what was happening when Nicky then yanked her cloud of frizz down and Urma Thurb pinned on the tiara. Jen felt like a lamb for the slaughter. She felt like an IDIOT. Everything hurt.

So they were all set! Something borrowed, something blue. They were ALL feeling a little blue, as they plodded to the horse and carriage: Jen was SCARED, Urma Thurb was missing her hubby, and Nicky had a hangover (they were also irritable from ENVY and PIQUE, like everybody else at a wedding).

Who wants to know anything about their doctor's LOVE LIFE? It's like having to think about your PARENTS fucking. Nonetheless, most of Dr Lewis's patients (the ones that were still ALIVE) were dutifully milling about the church. Martha was in the FRONT ROW, helplessly stirred by the organ. Dotted around elsewhere were Trevor, Catherine, Frieda, Jack, John, Janet, Sam, Sylvie, Marvin (without MAY), and others. (But no Virginia.) Francine, wearing a Jackie Onassis PURPLE number mit pillbox hat, was herding Dr Lewis's kids around the churchyard like little DUCKLINGS, searching for children's tombstones.

Dr Lewis circulated happily amongst his guests, quizzing them on ecclesiastical architecture and hymns until they were all eager for him to shut up and get married! But the women softened when he picked up their BABIES. What is it about the sight of a grown man holding a baby – of his OWN SPECIES – that moves people so? What is so REMARKABLE? Do they expect him to EAT it? We're not lions!

Finally, Jen and Roger stood at the altar, with Nicky all geared up to GIVE JEN AWAY. The ceremony was long and convoluted. Roger had opted for the Latin Mass, Communion wafers, Bath Olivers, and Jammy Dodgers. He exhausted everyone with his hymn choices and hymn MIX-UPS. They stood, they knelt, they sat down, stood again, knelt, sat down by accident, blushed, tipped OVER, collected themselves, sang, knelt, prayed, stood and sat. It began to feel like THE END OF THE WORLD.

Finally the priest started winding things up by asking if there were any objections to this match. If only he'd asked sooner – because there WERE!!! All those hymns were a big waste of time! A muffled sound was heard coming from the back of the church and a dark, wet, hairy, slimy purplish thing like a walking VULVA made her way slowly up the aisle. What base cunt was this? Bleeding, drooling, stinking, swelling – and yet the creature somehow commanded RESPECT.

When she reached the altar, she twisted round towards Dr Lewis and said, 'He can't get MARRIED – he's already married to ME!' And then she started to CACKLE, a laugh very similar to a SQUAWK. In spite of the VEIL which (as always) clouded her vision, Jen now saw that the interloper was none other than:

FRANCINE!!!

Jen looked over at Roger, who was OVER-QUIRKING. Jen had never SEEN such quirking! This was turning into a real quirking EMERGENCY. Then she fainted, an AVALANCHE of squashed tulle and taffeta and crêpe and lace and satin and DIADEMS, that covered the stone floor. There were people there, INSANE PEOPLE, who hoped Jen would do a SOMERSAULT, but they were disappointed. Her humiliation was restricted to lying like a flayed SHEEP, spread across the aisle, until fourteen or fifteen of the wedding guests recalled they had medical experience and rushed up to conduct First Aid on her.

Once she had been thoroughly resuscitated at least four times, Jen instinctively reached for her TIARA, as you do, but it was gone. Her WAIST was going too – some of the stays must have snapped. Jen desperately searched the crowd for Nicky and Urma Thurb, her ATTENDANTS, but they were nowhere to be seen! Probably laughing behind her back somewhere, at the MERINGUE OF THE FAMILY.

Roger was signalling her to get up. As always, his aloofness galvanised her. Jen stood. Roger grabbed her hand and beckoned the others to join them.

'You would not begrudge me this woman if you knew how I live!' said he, as he led a parade of colleagues and patients past the failing post office, the failing café, the failing fish shop, the failing school, the chemist's shop, the sweetie shop, the petrol station, the antique shop and various pubs, to the surgery. (They picked up a few more locals on the way.)

When they entered the house, Jen felt a strong urge to descend, ALONE, to her den to eat ICE CREAM. But Roger dragged her panting up the stairs with him. They climbed and climbed, followed closely by Francine and the kids, and then the rest of the crowd. Once in the attic, the two kids hid in the kitchen doorway, peeking out at the horde of visitors. They were ALWAYS standing in doorways, as if they had no right to enter a whole ROOM.

Those kids had learnt to live with a father who was OUT most of the time, a father who seemed to know nothing of joy, and a mother who was out COLD (recovering from her numerous BEAUTY TREATMENTS), a mother who, when conscious, was a MAD thing, dark, wet, stinky and slimy! With her they had often sat up late waiting for Roger to come, since he had declared that a HAPPY family EATS together (he too read *Take a Break*!). As a result of this edict, they often went to bed with *NO* supper. Edward and Adele had been quietly biding their time since the announcement of Dr Lewis's engagement, in the hope that Jen would inject some REGULARITY into the food sitch (she didn't look like she skipped too many meals).

Dr Lewis now spread his hands in a theatrical gesture of defeat. 'As you can probably see, I just can't cope any more,' he confided to the assembled throng.

No one could refute this judgement: everything in the flat seemed to be broken, burnt or WET, every door off its hinges, armchairs with no ARMS, tables lying on their sides, clothing, possibly VOMIT, in every corner. There was a STINK, a cloud of stinks, that included the Leaning Tower of Pisser and chip fat and waiflike children, and the stale fruity smell of the orange flight suit.

'Was there some kind of STRUGGLE here?' asked the priest, nominating himself, quite erroneously, as the ARBI-TER of everything.

'No, it just looks like this,' said Roger.

'So, does your wife live with you?' asked the nosy new postmistress. (But it WAS her business – she didn't want letters going astray!)

'She has to,' said Roger. 'I have to keep an eye on her at all times. She's NUTS. That's why I let her man the phone in the surgery.'

Everyone stared at Dr Lewis, trying to take this in.

'She went nuts at Disneyland. A few years ago.'

A murmur of sympathy rose from the crowd. They too had been to Disneyland.

'She went berserk on the plane home. Caught her own

reflection in the porthole – she thought she'd seen her MOTHER outside the plane. Threatened to kill all the children on board, didn't you, my love?' He turned to Francine, who was burbling to herself on the arm of a broken chair. He stroked her cheek but drew his hand back in a hurry when she tried to BITE it.

'What was the attraction, may I ask?' the priest enquired.

'What?'

'At Disneyland.'

'Oh, *Mr Toad's Wild Ride*,' Roger affably replied. 'It was *too* wild for Francine.'

'I like *Pirates of the Caribbean*,' said the priest. Everyone then started shouting out their favourite ride at Disneyland, their various DISAPPOINTMENTS at Disneyland, and the amount of DOUGH they'd sunk into Disneyland. Once the din had died down, Roger resumed his explanation (how he loved a crowd!).

'She's been making trouble for *days* about the wedding, I don't know why. Our marriage has been over for years! I found her trying to destroy the wedding dress last night! The trouble is, Jen reminds Francine of her MOTHER.'

Everyone was much *moved* by Dr Lewis's excuses. They were full of sympathy for the good doctor. Nobody cares about BIGAMY these days (they care a lot more about DISNEYLAND), and everyone wants to think well of their GP! Rising to the occasion, Francine stood on the chair and beat her breast, crying, 'My mother, my MOTHER!'

Jen, who had never been to Disneyland, was feeling rather SICK and not just because of the CUMMERBUND: she was thinking about the AEROPLANE, the one on which Roger had supposedly been Hero of the Hour! The woman he'd so effectively SUBDUED on the plane, it seemed, was his WIFE, the mother of his BRATS. Some hero. Sedating and tying up your own wife is the LEAST a man can do!

Jen might have been able to endure SOME of this, had she

not been trussed up like a big fat buttered stuffed oven-ready TURKEY in all those stays and the cummerbund, but they made her feel so OUT OF BREATH! Pushing her way past the priest, who got squished behind a door (as all promulgators of religion SHOULD be), she ran out into the hallway and down the stairs, JEN, who hadn't run willingly anywhere in years! Inevitably, she tripped on her dress. Down she spun, a barrelling croissant of centrifugal force. It was a long time before people could stop talking behind Jen's back about the sight of her toppling: red face, white dress, red cummerbund, white-stockinged thighs, red ASS, white shoes, red white red white red white. Like one big BREAST she bounced!

CIVILISATION

So now begins the lavish period of EXILE, in which Jane Eyre wanders starving across the MOORS, implausibly hooks up with some distant cousins, and considers marrying the sexless SINJUN and converting the INJUNS. All that stuff after the aborted wedding is a FIASCO – and it takes up a third of the book! It's the biggest black hole in English literature! Brontë's got the poignant childhood all sewn up, she's got ROCHESTER, who's sexy and moving, and she's got the passionate JANE who, innovatively, is not perfectly beautiful (though couldn't she have made her a bit UGLIER? Jane doesn't quite hate herself ENOUGH). And then she goes and BLOWS it, wantonly destroys her own BOOK with that hideously dull WILDERNESS year. WHY? What HAPPENED? Why didn't somebody STOP her? Such inordinate penitence for the sin of wanting a married man! (And all because of that Belgian PROFESSOR Brontë was so stuck on.) Charlotte, CHARLOTTE!

JEN'S exile will not be long or lavish – a mere two days! And there will be no STARVING nonsense – Jen has had the foresight to pack her tidy white pearl-beaded BRIDAL BAG with a SWITCH card, and she hasn't LOST it yet (Jen never mislaid a handbag in her life!). While everyone else in town is still gaping at Dr Lewis's domestic arena, Jen in her crumpled wedding dress stands outside the bank, trying to extract cash from the cash-point machine. TRIUMPH: money comes out. From there she heads for the train station.

Sensing that her preternatural calm is about to disintegrate, she rushes into the Ladies and there weeps for a considerable time. She thinks – but how dare we intrude on what Jen is thinking at such a juncture? Are we BARBARIANS? Are we BEASTS? Yes.

O the mind, mind has mountains; cliffs of fall FRIGHTFUL. Jen is in a spiral of self-hatred, she has reaped the WHIRLWIND by daring to love Roger Lewis. There is fission, there is fusion! Thoughts she usually buries so as to be able to FUNCTION, be SEEN, hold down a JOB, now surface in a MUSHROOM CLOUD of self-disgust. There is no HOPE. Her every mistake looms GARGANTUAN in her mind: Roger's coldness, Francine's perfidy, her brother's scorn, Urma Thurb's DEFECTION, her father's revulsion, her MOTHER's too (preferring DEATH to Jen). ALSO the girls at school who talked about Jen behind her back while she hid in a booth, the OSTEOPATH who fucked her senseless, the SERVING WENCHES who have thwarted her, the repugnance of FISH girls and the like, the BABIES she's killed, the cats she's kicked, the hapless Eakinses, the VEIL between herself and the world (Jen is well aware of it!), the huge LONELINESS OF LIFE, characterised by all the clandestine PANCAKES she's eaten, the garlic bread and buttered POTATOES, the apple CRUMBLES she's baked herself late into the night, the CHIMICHANGAS!

And her BODY, that endless fund of grotesquerie with its pockmarked pustuled droopy SKIN, the extravagant, hitherto UNHEARD-OF design of her BREASTS, her upper arms that flap in the wind, her WIND too (Jen is the main source of METHANE in the world), the Niagara Fall of CHINS and her stupid STUPID face, the smug mouth, dead eyes! The BURDEN of having bodies at all (including the problem of having to take HERS somewhere NOW), the HORROR, the TROUBLE they give us! Jen is not *immune* to the tragedies around her, the diseases; she's seen what they can do. MOMO syndrome. Eczema. Cirrhosis. Blindness. Dementia. NODULES.

She wails and wails! She cries for herself and for the WORLD, a world in which there are artificial limbs and plastic carrier bags and hiccups and JOBS and *Take a Break* magazine and the BUSH regime and the general indecision about SMOKING. These things will destroy us all!

She widens her scope to include just about EVERYTHING. Everything in the world makes her cry more and more, though she TRIES to stop. Trying to STOP makes her cry more! She weeps until she howls with LAUGHTER, which seems to her the saddest sound she's ever heard. She laughs until she CRIES again! But even in a crisis one is selective. Jen's meltdown excludes certain things: tulips, two-pound coins, book-binding, and the aurora borealis. Except that she's never SEEN the aurora borealis and she's always WANTED to see the aurora borealis and she probably never WILL see the fucking aurora borealis – so she cries about that too!

Mainly she weeps from lack of hope on a grand scale, GRAND OPERA disappointment. Jen has always been disappointed, as far back as she can REMEMBER (haven't we all?). And throughout her tears, she sees only one solution: Anna Karenina's. Jen's MOTHER's too: pitched past pitch of grief, women choose the phallic train to die by (a true admission of defeat).

But first Jen has to blow her nose. She blows and BLOWS it! Don't you wish sometimes that it would all just COME OUT – snot, spit, pee, shit, vomit, tears, sperm, blood – in one final SPASM of evacuation and LEAVE YOU BE? Or alternatively, that you could shove it all IN – food, water, alcohol, drugs, sounds, smells, sperm, tampons, EYE OINTMENT, asbestos particles – and be done with it? But it doesn't work! Always you need MORE.

She throws her wedding bouquet down the loo, there being no sign forbidding the disposal of wedding bouquets down the loo, and no wedding-bouquet INCINERATOR handy (though there SHOULD – women will be pissing on Jen's flowers for weeks to come!). Then she splashes water on her forehead FOR THE LAST TIME. She splashes it all over her FACE, but the tears still spurt. She dries herself on her veil, but still the tears spin out and plop on to the wide white satin LINTEL of her breasts which, so tightly and brightly swaddled, have merged pragmatically into one. Looking a little GREEN amid all that white, Jen wanders out on to the platform.

By the time a train appears in the distance she's calmer and PINKER, but still resolved on death, the only dignified way out of her present predicament. The GLADIATOR's way out. She steps bravely forward to meet her end. But her stupid dress gets caught by the leg of a bench! Jen battles with that bench as if it were a LION. It's clear from the start who the VICTOR will be, but it all takes too long! By the time she's pulled herself free from its claws and given the lion the *coup de grâce* with her HANDBAG, the train has already entered the station and is moving at a speed that lacks melodrama.

But it offers escape of a sort. On the spur of the moment, Jen decides to get on it! She doesn't care where it's going, so long as it takes her to a bigger railway terminus where there might be more HIGH-SPEED trains on offer: an Anna Karenina jump is not something you want to MUFF.

C-SHAPES

Jen heaves herself on to the train, but there's a TICKET COLLECTOR barring her way! Not just because she is a BRIDE IN DISARRAY, but because she has boarded the train via the FIRST-CLASS CARRIAGE. If ever there was a moment when a little ideological LENIENCE might not go amiss, this is IT. But no. The ticket collector launches into a TIRADE about the impudence of entering the first-class carriage when not in possession of a first-class ticket.

Jen asks if she can just walk *through* the first-class carriage to get to the low-class UNDERCARRIAGE. No. She then volunteers to get OFF the train and use another door, if it's not too late. But it IS: the train has started to move while they debate the rights and wrongs of entering a first-class carriage. I should be drinking CHAMPAGNE right now, Jen thinks. (CHEAP champagne.) In the end he gives in and allows Jen to proceed through the first-class carriage, but warns her not to annoy anyone, for the whole point of the first-class ticket RULE is to stop first-class passengers being annoyed. 'Don't disturb anybody,' he adds.

'I'll *try* not to,' Jen snaps, glowering at him. Then she stomps through the first-class area, smothering many in the many folds of her manifold finery, KICKING a few too (but they seem to LIKE it!). Soon enough, she's in a PLEB seat surrounded by pleb NOISE. Not only the deafening

ANNOUNCEMENTS at every station telling you where the fuck you ARE (but never WHY), and the Buffet Service Manager reminding you there's a BUFFET car on board serving light and dark drinks and high and dry snacks. But also all the people talking on their FUCKING mobile phones: I'm on the train . . . yes, the train . . . I'm calling from the train . . . we've just left . . . we'll be getting in at . . . the TRAIN, I TOLD you . . .

There's a guy opposite Jen eating CHEESY WOTSITS, his crunching RELENTLESS. Computer-game sounds, snippets of electronic SCARLATTI, abruptly truncated and then REPEATED. Elsewhere, the z-zz-zzzz-BOOMPH of somebody's Walkman. A woman behind Jen is talking on the phone to her hubby (?) about the ROUTE the train's taking and the loveliness of the DAY and how much she wishes he were there beside her now. The whole carriage has to LISTEN to this! She speaks Very Clearly, in a sort of KINDERGARTEN TEACHER voice. She's turning them all into her new baby class!

There IS a baby on board somewhere, a squalling, mewling, farting, stinking BABY. But Jen was one herself once, left to mewl and piss and fart in an empty compartment for hours (she still does so whenever she gets the chance!). As instructed by the woman behind her, she stares out of the window. Pheasant. Deer in a soggy field. Rabbits. Sheep. Clouds. Hills. Water. Sun. But Teacher Lady is strangely quiescent when they pass a pen full of PIGS. Perfect pigs – mit PIGLETS! They're dark and frisky, and the perfect pig SHAPE. What, hubby doesn't care about PIGS?

Looking across the aisle, Jen sees a girl engrossed in celeb magazines. And suddenly Jen is maddened by it all. Rising up out of her seat, she yells, 'Hey, we're supposed to be trying to have a CIVILISATION around here!' But it does no good! Nobody listens – nobody can HEAR her over the dreadful din. So she sinks back down and only now notices that the white metal back of the seat in front of her is adorned with the words:

I LIKE PUSSY

Jen wants to add 'I LIKE COCK', but she's scared of the ticket collector. He might see her and think she STARTED it. She doesn't want to be ARRESTED. On her WEDDING day!

GRAFFITI BRIDE CAUGHT
SCRIBBLING FILTH ON TRAIN

A large unaccompanied woman wearing a bridal gown illegally boarded a train via the first-class carriage and was later found defacing railway property with graffiti of an obcene and wholly uncalled-for nature.

She is being held in the slammer until someone can vouch for her, which is unlikely since she has no friends and is in fact motherless, fatherless, rootless, ruthless, angry and alone.

The appealing sound of the food trolley! But it rushes by without stopping! I should be eating CHICKEN ROULADE by now, Jen thinks, before falling into a deep, post-weep sleep. She's woken by a girl plopping clumsily into the seat beside her, KICKING Jen in the process. Why must people announce themselves this way? Jen wants to THROTTLE her. *I am going to have to kill you now.* The things we'd DO, if we knew we could get away with it. (The Roman emperors SHOWED us what we'd do and it ain't pretty!)

ROGUE BRIDE KILLS FELLOW PASSENGER
BECAUSE 'HUNGRY'

A big fat woman wearing an ill-fitting wedding dress struck without warning when a fellow passenger just happened to sit down next to her on a train.

> To the alarm of other passengers, the unarmed victim was beaten to a pulp in the unprovoked attack, then tarred, feathered, hung, drawn, quartered, and flayed.
>
> In her defence, the bride said she had been feeling 'a little hungry' at the time.

The image of the PASTA MACHINE Urma Thurb gave her as a wedding present comes into Jen's head. I WANT MY PASTA MACHINE! She feels like crying about the PASTA MACHINE now but CAN'T, because of a guy in front that won't stop PEEPING at her through the gap between the 'I LIKE PUSSY' seat and the window. Jen keeps catching his EYE, just ONE eye. It's disconcerting. To avoid him, she looks out of the window again.

Twilight. Damp stucco houses by a river. Probably NEVER dry out, stuck there on their dead end. But what do THEY know about DEAD ENDS? Black rushing water of the river. Above, a crescent moon. Below, the white C-shapes of foam as the water hits big rocks in the shallow riverbed. In the darkness all Jen can SEE are these C-shapes – like BREASTS – and the buttocklike clefts of hills. The body is our metaphor always for interpreting the world.

Jen has lost her appetite for suicide. She's too HUNGRY to DIE! All she wants now is a bed for the night, and something nice for supper. When the train starts to slow for the next station, she gets stiffly to her feet in her tight little white wedding shoes and stumbles towards the door. On the way though, she leans sweatily over the creepy Kindergarten Lady and says confidentially, 'The body is our metaphor for interpreting the world. Call your husband and tell him THAT, lady!' – before lugging her own sorry ass off the train.

THE WEDDING NIGHT

Jen found herself in the dark cold station of some small dark town. It felt like the NORTH POLE, or at least the ROOF OF EUROPE, whatever that is.

Outside the station she was immediately accosted by a sneering young man who'd spotted her huge white form in the darkness. He made some unintelligible comment about her HAIR. Jen would have punched him but she was reluctant to be punched BACK, alone with him there in the dark on the brink of time.

But within sight was the Station Hotel, so Jen hurried on over there and lunged through the doors, SWING doors like a Wild West SALOON. She was relieved to find that her accoster didn't dare follow her in – this hotel wasn't big enough for the two of them!

She rang the bell at the desk but no one came, so she followed the sound of chatter coming from the bar. Everybody shut up when Jen entered, like she was JESSE JAMES or something! The barman even stopped laughing at his own joke. Two old ladies having their dinner in a corner let the peas roll off their forks as they stared at Jen. Quick on the draw, she ordered a whisky, gulped it back and asked for another. 'Keep 'em comin, pardner!' she snarled. Cuz this was after all her rip-roarin', hard-shootin', darn-tootin' WEDDIN' DAY.

When she'd had about as much as a girl can take, of the whisky AND the stares, she asked the barman about a room for the night. He led her back to the reception desk where he suddenly became the Hotel Manager. Jen signed the book 'Loathe Self' and, in answer to his question, 'Any bags?' she mystifyingly replied, 'You mean ma GRIPS, mister? I travels light and I travels alone.' He made her pay in advance therefore, then took her upstairs through a hallway hotter'n Death Valley to a room colder'n a sheriff's balls or a hangin' judge's heart, all the time a-CHAWIN' on something. WHAT??

The room was without charm (Jen CHECKED it for charm but there wasn't any). And the WINDOW didn't shut. No wonder it was COLD in there! It looked out over a low flat roof (the roof of Europe?), on to which varmints of any kind could easily climb. It made Jen nervous, nervous as a prairie dog in a BUFFALO stampede! But it would have to do. Jen shat (yes, you have to shit even on your wedding day), blew her nose, cried, splashed water on her forehead and abstractedly examined her very own tiny bar of crappy hotel SOAP, before trundling back downstairs in search of food. The Manager was at his desk, whispering (about JEN?) to some FLOOZIE on the phone, some JEZEBEL. (Otherwise, Jen might have complained about the WINDOW.)

She strode nervously down the middle of the dark, deserted high street, like Gary Cooper, sensing she was being stared at from every dingy window. 'COME OUT, YOU COWARDS!' she yelled. The CHIP SHOP beckoned, a BEACON in the darkness! Jen burst through the door and ordered two large portions of chips and two pieces of FISH – it's the only way to ensure they don't skimp on the CHIPS. What did SHE care what they thought of her? Anyway, they probably thought she had a BRIDEGROOM waiting in the car somewhere.

BASHFUL BRIDE SLIPS OUT
FOR FISH AND CHIPS

A newlywed was left high and dry, tied to a four-poster in the Honeymoon Suite of the Station Hotel, when his wife of six hours suddenly dashed from the room!

Was she fleeing the Facts of Life? No, just getting fish and chips.

At a newsagent's she bought some o' them fancy EATIN' chocolates and some chawin' tobaccy. At an off-licence, low-cal white wine. She was carting her haul back to the hotel like a PACK MULE when she was again ACCOSTED by the impudent young man! This time he RAN at her. Men should never run at women (unless it's to SAVE them from CALAMITY). Jen headed him off at the pass and managed to skidaddle back inside the Bucket o' Blood Saloon before he could catch up with her. Vamoose, stranger! But she was now sure he would climb in through her window and MURDER HER IN THE NIGHT.

First though, she was going to shovel all her goodies down her throat! The chips were too PALE, the fish too greasy, but she ate them all the same. I want whatever I WANT today, it's ma weddin' day.

Jen falls asleep watching Meg Ryan play a DRUNK. It seems to go on for ever (Meg Ryan shows no mercy). When Jen wakes up, the TV's still on. She's confronted by MORNING NEWS on every channel, each with its own pair of male and female presenters – the nation cannot rise without these mummy and daddy figures barking at them. They're so RESTLESS: they can't sit still, and keep changing places during the ads, like TENNIS players. Clearly want to THUMP each other most of the time.

How cheerily they talk of dead, dying, bullied and obese children! The presenters seem to think themselves SUPERIOR to these children, because they SURVIVED childhood. Smirking away, they try to look stricken with concern but it's a struggle. CUT to a guy standing in front of the Old Bailey in the rain, gripping an enormous yellow umbrella, there at least four HOURS before judge, jury or PERPETRATOR, just to be able to say (at six in the morning): 'Live from the Old Bailey.'

Jen squirms back into her grubby dress and fiddles angrily with hooks and eyes, while Tony Blair drinks a cup of TEA and tries to look stricken about AIDS or rape victims or Chinese cockle-pickers or maybe even Abu Ghraib. This reminds Jen that she wasn't MURDERED IN THE NIGHT. No shoot-out, no posse, no lassoes, no coyotes. With her whole life seemingly still before her, she plods downstairs for breakfast.

Jen sits for some minutes being stared at by other guests before a waitress comes to take her order. The WORKS: kippers, bacon, eggs, sausages, beans, kidneys, mushrooms, tomatoes, black pudding, fried bread, chips, etc. In the meantime, juice, cereal, yoghurt, muffins, croissants, and soggy old tinned GRAPEFRUIT segments. A hero's breakfast! Jen eats as if somebody's DIED! CHOWS down. And *while* she eats she thinks about FRANCINE. The NERVE of the woman, betraying Jen for MONTHS with her simpering smiles and seeming DISCRETION, whilst secretly scuttling around DESTROYING EVERYTHING behind Jen's back. The LIES, the TEA, the CHUMMINESS, the GAMES she played! OK, the woman's NUTS, so she can't be blamed for any of it, but the DUPLICITY that lay behind that innocent-looking, if artificial, exterior!

Also, how exactly was Jen meant to fit into that domestic scene? Not one complete CHAIR to his name, unless you count the swivel chairs in the surgery! She knows Roger sends all his spare cash to *Médicins sans Frontières*, but a guy planning a *ménage à trois*, in fact a MENAGERIE, might at least provide a spot for your ASS . . .

* * *

Things that most people do with a SMILE, like serving you BREAKFAST and taking your hard-earned DOUGH, these people did WITHOUT one. It's a system! Jen had to eat amid frowns and stares.

'What? WHAT? You never seen a JILTED BRIDE before?' she screamed at the guy opposite, in her excitement dropping a whole grilled TOMATO on her dress. (Ah, the tomato.) She only quietened when more TOAST arrived, and more TEA. As she poured herself another cup, Jen suddenly thought she heard ROGER'S VOICE, calling, calling, calling her BACK to him! Her master's voice.

Was it ESP, or just some peculiarity of the TEAPOT?

THE MEANING OF LIFE

Jen didn't find the meaning of life that morning! Let us rejoin her in the AFTERNOON.

By now she was carrying two brass candlesticks and a big WOODEN thing. She'd been in a charity shop earlier, run by a guy with a very high voice. She was looking for cargo pants, but they didn't have any, and she was about to leave when the guy with the high voice offered her some candlesticks at a ROCK-BOTTOM PRICE! Then she made the mistake of asking about the big wooden thing in the window.

'Oh, *that* is a Shetland sweater-dryer,' he replied proudly.

Drying sweaters was obviously a BIG PROBLEM in the Shetlands, and pretty IMPORTANT. Jen thought it might come in handy for drying CARGO PANTS too! So here she was, the jilted bride with her loot. Naturally, she was causing a bit of a stir in the high street. People were mumbling and grumbling behind her back, as usual. Couldn't they leave her alone for ONE MINUTE?

But it turned out they WEREN'T mumbling about Jen. Her customary position in society had been USURPED by a NAKED MAN, who was wending his way down the street wearing only HIKING BOOTS and a HAT!

Children giggled as he passed, men scowled, and women smiled (women LOVE looking at naked men). Jen RECOGNISED him from a news report she'd seen that morning. He was visiting every town in Britain NAKED to spread his message about ACCEPTING THE BODY. His own body was of course not accepted anywhere – he kept getting ARRESTED. Maybe that was why he was tackling this town at such a pace. His long legs were much in evidence: Jen had to RUN to keep up!

'Look at us!' he yelled. 'We're killing ourselves with SELF-HATRED! Where does it get anybody? People still DIE. Millions die every DAY because we hate ourselves! DEMOCRACY'S dying because we hate ourselves!'

A few people clapped. The naked guy stopped so suddenly Jen almost bumped into him.

'Who do we think we're KIDDING anyway with all this secrecy about the human body?' he asked the crowd. 'Animals? CHILDREN? They have bodies too!' A police siren could be heard in the distance, but he seemed unperturbed. 'It's all wrong,' he declared as he started marching onwards again.

'Hooray!' Jen cried, waving a candlestick in the air. She had discovered a new HERO (her Hero slot was unoccupied at present). This was the first time in her life that Jen had been told not to HATE herself and she LOVED it!

A police car now swerved right in front of the naked guy, blocking his path. Three cops jumped out.

'You can't ban the human body,' the naked man declared as they handcuffed him. They led him through the crowd to the police car, amid a few boos. 'You can't crush the body!' he yelled. But they DID, getting him into the car. Then off they sped, three smiling policemen and A NAKED MAN IN CHAINS.

Outraged, Jen turned to a woman near her and said, 'Since when did the human body become illegal? I didn't know clothes were COMPULSORY, did you?'

But the woman stared at Jen with naked ABHORRENCE and crossed to the other side of the street. The rest of the townsfolk meekly dispersed. It was *High Noon* all over again!

COWARDS. You let ACCOSTERS OF WOMEN roam free but a nice NAKED guy has to be LOCKED UP. What a ONE-HORSE TOWN!

Someone had to carry on his good work! DUTY IS ALL. Jen was tired of secrets, secret eating, secret wives in the attic, the secrets of her body. She was tired of hating herself (REALLY tired of it). EVERYBODY gets to have a body, not just the BEAUTIFUL, not just those in FIRST CLASS. EVERY BODY is a legitimate example of the species! Not fair to treat a single one with disdain – not even JEN'S. The body is where all the LIFE is! Even sick bodies, old bodies. They're ALIVE. Every defect, every illness, springs from LIFE. Every body SPEAKS of life. Sitting up or lying down – LIFE. Rich or poor, fat or thin, fit or feeble – life. They're JAMMED RIGHT THROUGH with life. Friend or foe, liked or unliked – LIFE.

Your body is not something APART from you, something bad to be JUDGED, CRITICISED, SHUNNED. It's YOU, not discardable until death. It's not NOTHING. It's the ONLY thing there is.

DELIGHT in its survival, delight in it!

EPIPHANY IN THE BUSH

Following these thoughts to their logical conclusion, Jen ripped off her clothes in the middle of the sad little high street, relishing her release not only from all that TULLE, but from the tortuous and bewildering corsetry as well. She wanted OUT of this instrument of ENSLAVEMENT! She then strode BARE-ASSED through the town, holding her dress under her arm and waving the candlesticks above her head, like a Statue of Liberty that finally understood what liberty was all about! The price of freedom is to go UN-CLAD: freedom has BACKBONE, and that backbone's got to be VISIBLE.

People covered their ears, their EYES, as Jen drew near. But she didn't care. Equipped with nothing but a couple of candlesticks, a BIG WOODEN THING, and a few insights, she felt full of power and, curiously, LOVE. Outside a shop she gave all her coins to a tramp. The warmth of a beggar's hand!

Inside the shop, she sped about getting provisions. Other customers cowered in fear of Jen's elephantine form. The guy behind the counter picked up the phone to call the police. But Jen, with all the agility of new-found nakedness, bundled up her purchases, grabbed a small bottle of brandy for the road, threw the shopkeeper a £20 note and flounced out. The sight of THAT ASS caused a few people to faint. One had a heart attack! But Jen was OFF-DUTY. In fact, all her medical training now seemed a NONSENSE, an insult, a mockery of the body! So you get sick now and then, so what? The body deserves to be recognised and appreciated for what it IS, not castigated and penalised all the time for going wrong.

In the woods outside of town, Jen dumped her stuff under a bush and ran naked through the trees. Yes, Jen ran, HAPPILY ran, feeling the wind on her shoulders and her breasts flapping free, and nettles stinging her shins. IMMUNE to the sting, the sting of her TIMES – the hell-hole last breaths of the human race – she ran. She flung her floppy arms out and DANCED.

Lying on the ground afterwards, purple and panting, she looked up through the trees at the blue sky, not minding for once that it was sky-blue. She even listened to BIRDS. Jen had lost her VEIL: not just her *wedding* veil, but her veil of separation from the world! She felt for once AT ONE with things, with her body, and the species in which it seemed to have a home.

When it got dark, she lit the candles she'd bought for her candlesticks, and made a sort of TENT out of her wedding dress by draping it over the Shetland sweater-dryer (it was the best use that had ever been made of either item). Then she ate some bickies, smoked some ciggies, drank brandy, longed dimly for CANDY and fell asleep, her thorny head resting on a carpet of cummerbund.

BUGS came in the night and stared at Jen as she slept, wondering at this human who had discovered the meaning of life – the bugs thought THEY were the only ones who understood the meaning of life. ANTS crawled in a long line up Jen's thigh – word went out in Formic that they had found a marvellous new QUEEN. They all wanted to claim her for their own! Flies thought she was a FLY. And FOXES slunk by, pretending to know nothing of joy, but Jen really cheered all those creatures up! They had thought they were alone in the world.

The next morning, Jen hadn't LOST the meaning of life, but it no longer thrilled her quite as much. She was cold and it was raining. She couldn't ignore the possibility of HYPOTHERMIA. She was HUMAN after all: she needed food, shelter, newspapers, hot drinks, a JOB, contact with her own species, and a place to dump her stuff!

She went back into town to see the nice guy with the high voice and the bargains, swapped her dress for a hideous TRACKSUIT, which was at least warm, and watched without regret as her wedding dress sank into a big catatonic heap in a corner, still bearing her impress.

She caught the next train home – to ROGER. Out of the window, the landscape seemed dizzyingly alive. Jen thought she saw molehills creeping sideways! They definitely moved a BIT. And after the rain cleared, the wet trees twinkled at her, PRISMATICALLY. Their leaves dripped with COLOUR, blue, green, purple, red, gold. They flashed at her like XMAS-tree lights! This must be what Xmas-tree lights are BASED on, Jen thought: wet, sparkling trees.

Finally the world was REAL to Jen, and open for INSPECTION. She was PART of it, a body in her own right. Neither inferior nor superior, just EQUAL – as we all are.

A PERFECT PIG

Jen returned from her days in the wild a WRECK: cold, wet and starving (though I PROMISED there would be no starving!). She looked at the attic windows and wondered if Roger was up there enduring the indignities of FAMILY LIFE. But she couldn't save him tonight. (Maybe tomorrow.) All she wanted to do right now was find that PASTA MACHINE Urma Thurb had given her!

There were signs of much coming and going in Jen's dungeon, perhaps to be expected after a wedding, especially an INCOMPLETE one. All the presents were stacked in a messy pile in a corner of the living room and, weirdly, all Jen's little colourful RUGS were gone, the ones she'd paid for with her OWN MONEY. Who'd taken them? FRANCINE?

Jen rooted around like a perfect PIG in the present pile, like the pigs she'd seen from the train (energetically). But she couldn't find the PASTA MACHINE. Fuck Urma Thurb! She must have CONFISCATED it on the grounds that there had been no wedding! But no, finally she FOUND it, at the very bottom of the heap (the back bottom, not the front).

Jen immediately set to work making the dough. According to the accompanying LEAFLET, you could make any shape you WANTED with this thing: it was a state-of-the-art NOODLER! The dough had to cool before she could cut it up. So Jen was planning to have a nice hot steaming soak in her JACUZZI while she was waiting. But when she went into the bathroom she found the jacuzzi covered in reddish SLIME. This was worse than ANY of Francine's previous bath rings! It looked like she'd been trying to create a new SPECIES in there, or make her own CLONE.

Seized by an odd revulsion (odd in a NURSE), Jen scrubbed and disinfected her jacuzzi. Then, with Dionne Warwick warbling in the background and candles in her candlesticks dribbling on to the rim of the bath, Jen finally BUBBLED, her body again at one with the world. *What the world needs now is love, sweet love*! WHILE she jacuzzied, Jen tried to LIKE herself by thinking of the life in every inch of her body, the MANY inches of it. *We don't need another mountain*! But it wasn't easy: the bubbles made it hard to concentrate.

She padded, naked and PROUD, into her bedroom to get her favourite nightie, a barrel-shaped expanse of flannel: she didn't want to catch PNEUMONIA. But Jen had a terrible shock when she reached her bedroom. All the walls were bare, bare as her ASS! The HANDBAGS were gone! All of them! Her mother's, with its pretty gold chain; Urma Thurb's (full of precious junk); the Lady Reporter's; the one Jen had designated as FRANCINE'S (actually much NICER than Francine's real bag); Martha the Orgasmic Woman's monstrous bundle of silken folds; even the SPORRAN and the antique MEDICAL BAG Jen had assigned to ROGER – GONE, all gone! The accumulation of a LIFETIME, a lifetime's GRUDGES and DISILLUSIONMENT, cunt-study and collapse, the numberless numb longings and leanings of loneliness!

She instantly guessed the CULPRIT of course. But still, the THOROUGHNESS of the operation appalled her. Nicky usually just snatched her BEST stuff, he didn't do HOUSE CLEARANCES. And WHY? Nicky had no use for HANDBAGS. Maybe he was jealous of Jen for nabbing a DOCTOR? But Nicky had had a million of them! Doctors were

CRAZY about him! Maybe he was angry that he'd been dragged to a godforsaken rural backwater for NOTHING. But LOTS of weddings never happen – that's no excuse for stealing HANDBAGS!

Foaming with rage she thundered into the kitchen, all her new-found CONTENTMENT shattered! Nicky had stolen that too! Not just her HANDBAGS, but her fucking TRANSFORMATION! Naked in her kitchen, Jen made pasta in the shape of Nicky's BONES: femurs, ulnas, fibulas, clavicles, and skull. FUCK THE BODY (Nicky's anyway). With sinister glee, she threw the ossified noodles into a big pot of boiling water, scalding her belly in the process. But who cared about Jen's belly? NOBODY.

She ate Nicky's BONES and Nicky's BLOOD (passata) and Nicky's DANDRUFF (Parmesan), then went to bed in her denuded room and nudely SLEPT, alone in the world – but bolstered by carbohydrates.

BACK TO NORMAL

Jen turned up for work the next morning as if nothing had happened! Roger was THRILLED, Francine less so. Francine thought she'd seen the LAST of Jen, Francine thought she'd WON. But Francine had to eat HUMBLE PIE (Jen made it for her out of some old coelacanth she had in the fridge – it tasted DISGUSTING).

Roger took Jen out to lunch in his Jag! Jen felt relaxed with him at last, for the FIRST TIME, and not just because of that upholstery. There were no SECRETS between them any more. Also. she had a new magnanimous approach to things since her epiphany. As they drove along she told Woger she had discovered the meaning of life. He told her about his WIFE.

According to Roger, he WAS the Hero of the Hour, for putting up with Francine all these years, never a leisure moment, never a day without DUTY. It was because of her freak-out on the plane that he had had to take this job in a rural backwater where no one knew who they were, so as to protect Francine from cops, shrinks, HER mother, HIS mother, and various busybodies.

'The trouble is, she thinks she looks like her mother, and she can't BEAR to look like her mother! So it's just one beauty treatment after another, a bit of plastic surgery here, eyelash-tinting there. This is why I have no money! It all goes on colonically irrigating my wife!'

He'd had to buy OUT for the boob job, the face-lift and the liposuction, but was able to do her collagen and Botox injections himself at the surgery. Francine's lunacies were mostly brought on by Botox botch-ups and collagen catastrophes.

'If I OVERDO the lips, or UNDERDO the forehead, she rampages around setting fire to things!' he told Jen. He and Francine were forever battling about the exact amount of beauty she REQUIRED.

Now he apologised for everything, for the way Francine had wrecked the wedding, *and* the wedding dress, and besmirched Jen's jacuzzi (JEN brought this up). He apologised for being MARRIED to Francine, for having KIDS with Francine, and for slightly misleading Jen about Francine's precise role in the household. In fact, it was all FRANCINE FRANCINE FRANCINE, until he also apologised for having a small PIMPLE below his left eye (only temporary). Roger wasn't quite in ROCHESTER'S league – he wasn't BLIND or ruined, his wife wasn't DEAD, and there was no big DOG accompanying him everywhere (unless you count that Jag), but there was just about enough pathos about the guy to mollify JEN. *Enough of zis talk*, she was thinking, *take off your clothes*!

They went to an idyllic country PUB (at last), as in doctor–nurse books! Roses, thatched roof, and TROUT in a stream or an ascending SERIES of streams, into which the fish were divided according to size, all waiting dutifully to be EATEN. But Jen and Roger didn't eat them. Too many BONES – Jen had eaten enough bones the night before, and neither of them was in the mood to perform the Heimlich manoeuvre that day.

FAT FIANCÉE SAVED BY HEIMLICH
MANOEUVRE – ONLY TO DROWN
LATER IN TROUT STREAM

Instead, they sat by the fire and ate steak-and-ale pie and drank Guinness. It would have been DREAMY if Roger could only have shut up about FRANCINE!

'As long as I make sure she has no access to knives, scissors, razors, guns, machetes, matches, poisons, and large hunks of wood, she's really quite manageable,' Roger explained to Jen. 'And, on the plus side, she's a great receptionist, and that saves me money!' (He'd been planning to stop JEN'S salary too after they got married!)

'All she ever does is tell people to go to hell,' Jen reminded him.

'Yeah, that's right. She's GREAT at it!'

A little later, Jen surfaced from deep inside her second bowl of rhubarb-and-ginger crumble to ask, 'But what do you expect us to do NOW, live in HARMONY sharing the HOUSEWORK, like some kind of HAREM?'

'Oh no, of course not!' said Roger (though he HAD expected that). 'I was planning to move Francine down to the basement as soon as you move upstairs. She's always been keen on that jacuzzi –'

Roger just wanted things back to normal, with Jen catheterising people on command and letting him tie her up whenever he felt like it.

BACK TO NORMAL. What an effort that is! Think of all the people in India, China, Finland, Turkey, Brazil and IRAQ, all trying to get BACK TO NORMAL. It's NORMAL to be trying to get back to normal! Dr Lewis sped along curvy country lanes, Jen by his side, just two more wretches seeking banality.

But when they reached the surgery, Jen marched straight to Francine in her station and SPUN her chair so fast the bottle of nail polish Francine was using at the time fell from her grasp, along with her big greasy old HANDBAG. As Jen had always suspected, Francine's beauty arsenal was elaborate. Out of the handbag fell:

1 powder compact
1 tube concealer cream
1 jar fake-radiance gel
1 tube haemorrhoid cream
1 pair tweezers
1 old Kleenex
4 tampons
12 Q-Tips
1 watercolour kit
1 pack notelets
1 box confetti (unopened)
1 bag sweeties
1 small bottle Kiehl's Blue Lotion
mascara
6 shades eyeshadow
1 set earplugs
1 fold-up rainhat
wallet
1 video-rental card
loose change
keys
1 box matches
1 pack ciggies
2 or 3 mirrors (1 broken)
7 years' bad luck
18 different nail polishes
1 box nail polish removal pads
1 jar aspirin
3 pens
1 gun
Jane Eyre
curling tongs
1 piece souvenir petrified bark
2 old buttons
2 knitting needles

knitting
1 pack playing cards
1 carton Ribena
1 metal nail file
1 photo album, containing before-and-after pictures
 of various types of plastic surgery
1 jar Vitamin C
4 safety pins
3 unmatched earrings
1 mobile phone
1 KitKat
CD Walkman
CDs
6 lipsticks
1 ancient free sachet camomile tea
3 periwinkle shells

It is most EMBARRASSING to have the contents of one's handbag exposed to public view. It's like performing an unexpected BACK-FLIP with no KNICKERS on! Nobody's quite ready for it. But Francine was too busy trying to regain her equilibrium (no small task) to care. Meanwhile Jen collected Francine's keys, tweezers, matches, knitting needles, nail file, safety pins (for SAFETY'S sake) and gun from the floor and tucked them into her own handbag. (She WANTED to take the KitKat but didn't!)

'I'm confiscating these,' she bellowed at Francine, but Francine didn't seem to NOTICE. She went right back to answering the phone in her usual discouraging tone: 'Why, you scum-sucking twerp!' she yelled. 'You expect us to do something about your disgusting little AILMENT? Are you mad?'

Things really were back to normal.

Out in the corridor (ninety-eight), Jen waved the nail file at Roger and said sternly, 'She could do some damage with this.'

'Yeah, to her cuticles!' he quirked, but he was quite taken

with Jen's new authoritative air. It stirred in him thoughts of SUBDUING her with yards of FLEX.

They went straight to the bedroom, where Roger commiserated about the mysterious disappearance of the handbags. 'What do you make of it?' Jen asked him. But Roger didn't know WHAT to make of it. Gone was his harem!!

They fucked like never before. No need for flex, only FLEXIBILITY. The veil had been torn from Jen's eyes! Forget eyes, her CUNT was now the window to her soul, her cunt was her CORE. Jen was open to the WORLD in some new way. She came as soon as Roger TOUCHED her, and *continued* to come, to a rhythm all her own that took her over and HIM, and made them sway and scream. It filled Jen with LOVE and SORROW, sorrow for the WORLD.

It was DEEP, it was ROUGH, this mating. Jen felt like some kind of MATA HARI, sexually cruel and powerful. She felt like she could take over the world, straddling the GLOBE, as if it were one of those big rubber exercise balls, IMPALING herself on the North Pole as she bounced up and down.

JEN was the new orgasmic woman of the district! SHE deserved the orgasm award. Hers was the coming of the APOCALYPSE! She was all CUNT, the embodiment of female murk, and all she wanted was Roger's cock in her, day in, day out. Like a big black hole she sucked him in, her astronaut.

INSULTS TO THE BODY

Jen had always thought of BUGS as a BAD thing. But now she noticed the air wouldn't be so NICE without the occasional tiny shiny BUG fluttering around in it. Bugs are like SNOW: they give the air volume and meaning! (Their BUZZING's good too.)

It was still warm enough to swim in the stream at the bottom of the gorge, a popular place on sunny days. Jen swam NAKED, and tried to convince others to join her! The main reason people LIKE swimming after all is that it's a chance to get naked, or nearly naked, with other people. Apart from eating, fucking, buying furniture, or seeing the DOCTOR, swimming is one of the few occasions when everybody can mutually acknowledge that the body EXISTS.

But professionally, Jen was in turmoil. Her nursy duties were increasingly in conflict with her new philosophy of life. Most medical practices now seemed to her a hysterical OVER-REACTION to illness, an insult to the body, impatiently interfering in private matters that would probably sort themselves out in their own good time. Jen freely told anyone who'd listen, the biggest secret of the medical world: a lot of ailments, if left alone, go away!

She wanted people to stop KICKING themselves for being ill, stop BLAMING themselves and being blamed by OTHERS (it's the fear of being REVILED for being sick that keeps women scampering to the doctor all the time!). She no longer enjoyed thumping lung patients on the back to make them cough and cry, nor renewing prescriptions for things that were more EMBARRASSMENTS than diseases. So she took everybody off their HRT and tranquillisers. Thanks to Jen, that rural backwater was getting a lot less tranquil: the joint was JUMPING. One by one, Jen suggested to people that they give up their body-hatred and squeamishness and, unsurprisingly, they LIKED the idea.

Any minute now that REPORTER BITCH would be back, writing a story on the village where naturism was rife and insurrection in the air! No doubt she'd attribute it all to the WATER SUPPLY or something, but it was Jen, JEN, who had changed – and that whole rural backwater had had to change with her, she was so Mata Hari-esque!

NAKED NURSE TAKES THE PLUNGE

'Skinny-dipping' is not just for the skinny, apparently. A very fat nurse, some might say a woman almost too fat to *be* a nurse, has begun a campaign to get her patients out of their beds and out of their clothes!

On sunny autumn days the local bathing-hole now churns with a hellish mass of heaving heathen forms who show no sign of shame. The police have been notified.

Jen's sabotage didn't end there. Her GLEE SPREE included (HAD to!) the liberation of the CUNT. No more hiding in basements, in euphemisms, in PANTY-HOSE, no more sanitary-napkin CONUNDRUMS and Smear Test nonsense, no more SUBSTITUTES (all her handbags were GONE anyway), the cunt wants to LIVE! When women came to see her now about the curse, the curse of having a CUNT, Jen set to work filling them with PRIDE in their PUSSIES. Most cunt pains and problems stem from self-loathing: women are always convinced they have something wrong with their genitalia, in fact that they have the WRONG GENITALIA. Jen was able to assure them otherwise.

She explained for instance that the vagina isn't just a passive TUBE at the service of sperm and babies, but a complicated sperm/germ SORTING system (It's a system!) with BIG PLANS and pleasures, PARADES, fireworks, hunting horns! Nor is the clitoris just a BUTTON for men to press, like calling a LIFT or letting off a nuclear BOMB. It's large and wishbone-shaped, its legs encircling the vagina. This (along with their other erogenous zones and extensive reproductive capabilities) explains why women like SEX so much. Women like sex much more than MEN!

Men think sex is all about THEM and what THEY want! They've had this wrong for THOUSANDS OF YEARS!! They think they're here to RUN THE SHOW, fix light bulbs, make MONEY, take out the trash. But their only real BIOLOGICAL purpose is to make women happy. THIS is what men were DESIGNED for. NOT to mock, tease, torment, exploit, deprive, baffle, belittle and BETRAY women but to attend, consistently and conscientiously, to FEMALE SEXUAL PLEASURE.

Women can do all that OTHER stuff by themselves!

Jen's views had quite an impact. She explained sex so well to one young couple (who'd been trying to deflower a BELLY BUTTON for months), that the girl immediately became pregnant and needed an abortion! But at least they were now fully aware of the CUNT. Jen was reminding a whole rural backwater it had GENITALS (a revelation for many).

Roger was not always available at this time. He had his Air Ambulance work and the Munchausen's cases (his miscarriages of justice), and he had even embarked on a little redecorating in the consulting room. The guy had HOBBIES, what can you do? And his patient-load, as always, was a perpetual nuisance.

FRED, for instance, had a STIFF NECK, which made him

tilt his head all the time. He had recently built himself a modernistic house, full of odd angles. It wasn't clear whether building it had CAUSED the stiff neck, or the already awkward angle of Fred's head had caused him to build such a HOUSE! He was forever painfully peering out of his weird windows. His WIFE had a sore SHOULDER. Dr Lewis's solution? Aspirin.

Roger was particularly annoyed with MRS PAMPOLINI at the moment, because she was FAT (he was annoyed with her NAME too: even that seemed fat!). Dr Lewis was convinced that fatness KILLS, that being fat is degenerate, dangerous and disobedient. He was mistaken of course: fat people outlive their doctors every day! But that didn't matter to Dr Lewis. It's FASHIONABLE to make people feel like CRAP about being fat – and he was the guy to do it! (Curiously, JEN's fatness had never bothered him – but she wasn't a PATIENT.)

Unfortunately, in Mrs Pampolini's case, there WAS some justification for his disapproval: she was diabetic. The thing was, Mrs Pampolini was always cooking up big FAMILY FEASTS for herself and the other Pampolinis. As a result, she often had to be rushed to hospital in a COMA. Dr Lewis had scolded and scolded her about this. He had even thrown his hands up in the air and slapped them down on his desk, in a peevish way he had of showing displeasure. But STILL she cooked and ate her way into medical emergencies. So he handed the case over to Jen.

Jen visited Mrs Pampolini at home and watched her cook. Jen also had to stay and eat the feasts so that she could advise Mrs Pampolini on which items to avoid. It worked! Mrs Pampolini stopped snacking on the wrong stuff and JEN got to eat:

vitello tonnato alla Milanese
petti di pollo farciti di carciofi
risotto giallo con costolette di maiale

quaglie nel nido
gamberi imperiali in salsa all'abruzzese
agnello arrosto alla moda del rinascimento
coniglio con le cipolle e funghi al funghetto
zampone allo zabaione
seppie ripiene coi piselli (sea sausages!)
involtini di peperoni
vignarola
castagnaccio
castagnole con la ricotta
and once, a whole BOMBA DI PANNA!

Duty is all.

Jen's new magnanimity even stretched to KIDS. For years Dr Lewis had been dosing AMY, a twelve-year-old epileptic, with some heavy-duty drug she didn't NEED, manufactured by a company WE CANNOT NAME. Amy was now WASTING AWAY. Dr Lewis said she was a MALINGERER, and she should just eat more. Even when Amy started to HALLUCINATE, he claimed it was nothing to do with the epilepsy drug. But Jen REBELLED and told Amy's parents to take her to hospital, where Amy died soon after. Doctors at the hospital attributed the child's death to the EPILEPSY MEDICATION she'd been on, but STILL Dr Lewis refused to believe this. HIS idea was that Amy's mother had STARVED her. (Mothers are the worst. They are the lowest of the low.)

'Be sensible,' he said to Jen. 'Which is more likely?'

Jen even took an interest in ROGER'S kids now, and included them sometimes in her activities. She fed them pasta in the shape of all the animals they'd never had as *pets* (dogs one day, cats, mice, hamsters, turtles or budgies another), and took them skinny-dipping in the stream. They were both most interested to hear what Jen had to say about ANATOMY: Adele proved a keen pupil of the vagina. Sadly for Edward, there was not so much to SAY about the penis.

But in the evenings, when the Lewis family, quite unlike the pampered PAMPOLINIS, was gathering yet again for one of their grim and grimy suppers (or no supper at all), Jen was racing naked through the gorge ALONE! Zinging with LIFE, she gorged on the gorge. The MOON didn't hold back on her. It was deaf, but only slightly aloof.

She was on her way to the stream one day, wearing a towel so as not to startle anyone, and lugging a basket full of Mrs Pampolini's spinach-and-ricotta CALZONI, and a bottle of wine (to take the chill off after the swim), when she found her path blocked by POLICE TAPE. Furious, Jen called out to two policemen standing near by, 'Hey, you're not banning SWIMMING now, are you?'

But they didn't seem to HEAR her, they were too busy SNIGGERING together about something. It was the kind of giggle NURSES reserve for the frayed and beshitted UNDIES of people who've died under BUSES. Now Jen was really alarmed!

'What's going on?' she asked sternly.

The policemen stared at her. Then one said, 'Body's been found.'

'What! WHERE?'

'Down there,' he said, pointing into the depths of the gorge. 'Or part of one anyway.'

'Stuck in a handbag!' the other volunteered, before they both creased over in a fit of hysterics and had to go huddle behind a tree.

Jen had never liked laughing policemen (she didn't like that SONG either). Nor did she like her gorge defiled with DEATH GOO. She trudged glumly back up to the surgery, hoping Roger would be there. He was! Revolving in his swivel chair and drinking a vast quantity of COCOA.

'There are policemen down below,' Jen announced.

Suspecting her of euphemism, Roger checked Jen's front bottom for policemen.

'In the GORGE,' she told him.

Ditto.

'OUTSIDE!'

Roger stiffened.

'They've found a BODY.'

'Well, that is what they're trained to do, of course,' said he, before pulling Jen down with him on to the floor and climbing on top of her. It was always quite a climb.

A SORT OF APOLOGY

The British LOVE a nice little murder! They're SUCKERS for it. Don't they ever realise how CORRUPT they are? It's almost impossible to sell a NOVEL these days unless it's got a MURDER in it! I know we've had plenty of murders in here already, but they weren't GORY enough to sell BOOKS and I'm SICK of not selling books, sick of people asking me why I don't write a THRILLER or something with a real STORY that SELLS, sick of reclusively writing these strange little books and then being told NOT to write them but to write NON-FICTION instead, the most POINTLESS, MEANINGLESS, TRUTHLESS, TOOTHLESS pursuit in the world! All because FICTION'S gone out of FASHION. The fickle public, brought up on REALITY TV, don't know what to MAKE of fiction any more, they don't know what it's FOR.

But what do *I* care about FASHION, holed up in my little EYRIE eating matzos and confronting my SELF-HATRED every day (or every other day)? Why don't people just LAY OFF, have a little HEART? Why don't they *APPRECIATE* me and my battle with self-loathing, which should be instantly *REWARDED* with LOVE and CASH! Why can't they give me more than I DESERVE, just for a little while? Why is it only GOOPS and IDIOTS – thriller writers and people who write about SALT or the POTATO – that get overpaid? Reading that stuff is like being DUPED, like being told what to THINK. It is a kind of PURGATORY.

I figure there's enough murder in my present tale to keep me in clover for the rest of my days, enough murder to satisfy ANYBODY. So here goes.

SOFT TISSUES

Bits of body were found all over the gorge in the ensuing days, tucked inside a great variety of handbags! The gorge proved the perfect receptacle for RETICULES: it hid them well. But once the police started looking, the horror-handbags seemed to nestle in every nook and cranny. A heart fell from a pink patent-leather handbag, when a policeman dragged it out of a hole in a tree. A foot peeked out of a navy-blue bag, betrayed by the glint of its pretty gold-chain handle; in an inner pocket was a matching LARYNX. Hastily buried under a gorse bush was a sparkly party bag; inside it they found a hunk of skin covered with pubic hair. Two skulls bobbed amongst ducks in the stream.

Oh, the body can be thoroughly destroyed! We're always thinking up new ways to do it. The things we've come up with! There's no GETTING AWAY from the GAS CHAMBERS or the Roman amphitheatres, or Hiroshima and witch-hunts and amputations and beheadings and massacres, no hiding from it! We all take note. We NOTICE how the human body has been treated, the dignity or lack of it. (We even care if people are BURIED right.) A collective HISTORY of misuses of the body is being written in all our heads ALL THE TIME, and it ain't pretty.

The bodies in the gorge had been thoroughly mutilated and strewn far and wide. The police never managed to find all the pieces: it was like putting a second-hand JIGSAW PUZ-

ZLE together – a frustrating task. But eventually they established that they were dealing with the remains of two bodies, one male, one female.

From Body No. 1 (female) they assembled:

the head
the right upper arm
the left upper arm
the left forearm and hand
the right lower leg and foot
the left leg and foot
the left thigh
the right thigh

From Body No. 2 (male):

the head
the chest
the back
the pelvis
the right humerus
the left humerus (tags of skin attached)
the right forearm and hand (portions of fingers removed)
the left forearm and hand (portions of fingers removed)
the right femur (with tags of adherent tissue)
the left femur
a portion of tissue (fat and muscle) with right kneecap attached
the right lower leg and adherent bone of foot (astragalus)
the lower left leg
the left foot (mutilation of toes)

Various miscellaneous parts turned up over the next few weeks:

the heart of Body No. 2
the brains of Body No. 1
the tongue of Body No. 1
the tongue of Body No. 2
the larynx of Body No. 1
the larynx of Body No. 2
the thymus gland of Body No. 2
the lungs of Body No. 2
the rectum of Body No. 2
the bladder of Body No. 2
the penis of Body No. 2
the scrotum of Body No. 2
the breasts of Body No. 1
the uterus of Body No. 1
the mons veneris of Body No. 1

According to police, the remains represented two adults, well developed and well nourished. The dismemberment of each had been effected by disarticulation through the joints and through the spinal column. There was no evidence of the use of a SAW.

There had been extensive removal of any soft tissues which might have helped in the determination of the cause of death, also removal of personal characteristics that might have facilitated identification, though the left arm of Body No. 1 still showed four vaccination marks.

The trunk of Body No. 1 was missing altogether, along with practically all the soft tissues clothing the right thigh, and soft tissues from other parts of the body. The terminal half of the distal phalanx of the right hand was also missing, as were almost all the organs of the chest and abdomen. In view of this, it was impossible to ascertain the cause of death.

With Body No. 2, the right foot, portions of the toes of the left foot, and portions of all of the fingers were missing, along with most of the soft parts and abdominal organs. The likely cause of death: asphyxia.

An examination of the hairs available indicated that the general colour of the hair of Body No. 1 was light brown and, in the case of the hairs from the front of the left ear, light brown with fairish tips. The hair from Body No. 2 was medium brown on the right side of the head, but the eyelashes were dark brown. The hair on a portion of vulval cleft was of medium brown colour – WHAT, you don't want to hear about VULVAL CLEFTS? Pah! You asked for murder and you got it!

The police estimated that the dissection of the bodies had taken place within a few hours of death, and concluded that the task of dismemberment and mutilation was likely to have presented difficulty to anyone without skill, anatomical knowledge, and suitable instruments. But, with these, the bodies could have been divided into the parts as found in about eight working hours. (Or QUICKER, with the right POP MUSIC.)

The bodies. After death, your body isn't YOU any more, but it still BELONGS to you: *his* body, *her* body. People say, 'His body arrived at the cemetery,' and you want to say, but where is HE and why doesn't he come and take that body of his HOME where it belongs? The bodies in the gorge had both had previous occupants: Body No. 1 was Urma Thurb's, Body No. 2 was Nicky's. The police identified them with ease, after pinning the time of the murder down to the day after Jen's WEDDING, which Urma Thurb and Nicky were known to have come from afar to attend.

Weddings are the cause of all human misery.

THE USUAL SUSPECT

Suspicion of course fell on JEN: she was FAT, she was an outsider, she lived BELOW GROUND and wore CARGO PANTS, her hair was a jungle and her body as vast and threatening as the MASSIF CENTRAL, the prairies of Oklahoma, or the Steppes of Russia (people could HEAR her step for miles!). This is just what such creatures do, this was JUST LIKE such creatures: they steal into a rural backwater and make murder and mayhem!

The reasons the *police* gave for suspecting Jen in the 'Bodies in the Glen' case, as it came to be known (thanks to the plucky REPORTER BITCH, who covered the story in the local paper), were as follows:

1. Nicky and Urma Thurb were the only guests Jen personally invited to the wedding.
2. Jen made no attempt to communicate with either of them after the wedding fiasco, suggesting she knew already that they were dead.
3. There were signs of estrangement between Jen and her brother: a whole history of rivalry and, more recently, discord over the sale of the family flat.
4. Urma Thurb had in fact FIRED Jen from her job on the Children's Ward, she didn't just QUIT.
5. There were traces of both victims' blood in Jen's base-

ment flat, and on several small colourful rugs belonging to Jen, found in the glen. Traces of blood and DNA evidence were also discovered in acid stains in and around her jacuzzi.

6. All the handbags used to conceal the crime had belonged to Jen – and THAT'S A LOTTA HANDBAGS!

The MOTIVE? Psychotic rage against these two intimate witnesses of her wedding mortification.

Aw, suspects, motives, alibis! The police make it all sound so simple, and so DULL. They reduce any tragedy to TEDIUM, drain everything of meaning.

Since Jen knew SHE hadn't done it, she quaked in her bed wondering who HAD, and fearing she would be next! She suspected FRANCINE, and thought with horror of Francine IN HER FLAT, cutting up the bodies and dumping them into the jacuzzi for an ACID BATH. Francine was just DETERMINED to wreck Jen's pleasure in that jacuzzi!

When the police first came to interview Jen in her dank and fetid little office (clearly the office of a MURDERESS, they all thought), Jen was quick to lay the blame on Francine. But the police weren't INTERESTED in Jen's theories! The police thought Jen was lacking in nursy COMPASSION, trying to frame a LOVE RIVAL of somewhat unsound mind. Also, madwomen in the attic are a literary cliché, and the police HATE books! They carried on with their questioning of JEN.

'Why did you make no attempt to contact either your brother or Urma Thurb after the wedding?'

'They didn't phone ME! I thought they could at least have sent a CONDOLENCE card or something, but when they didn't I just assumed they were cross with me. I didn't want to bother them.'

Jen wanted to know why TONY had never called to find out where Urma Thurb had got to. But Tony had had a calamity of his own: while trying to fix a LIGHT BULB, he had fallen down the hospital's grand Victorian stairwell and hit his head! The idiots at the hospital sent him home with CONCUSSION, and the poor fellow died in his bed, not long before the police turned up to tell him his wife had been dismembered and deposited in a GLEN.

'It was very romantic,' one policeman remarked. 'He probably died about the same time SHE did.' (A policeman's job is macabre; it makes them sentimental.)

'Well, what about Nicky's colleagues at the dentist's?' Jen asked. 'Surely they noticed when he didn't come back to work.' But then she remembered how often Nicky was away. He was always going to Belize or Bermuda, or health farms in TEXAS. His colleagues were accustomed to his long absences. And now he would NEVER come back. Being ELUSIVE is one thing, but DEAD? Who KNOWS how long the moment of dissolution may be, or how terrible?

'Why didn't the people who run the B & B say anything?' Jen asked. 'They must have noticed that Nicky and Urma Thurb never came back to collect their stuff!'

But the policemen explained that the B & B couple hadn't wanted to worry Dr Lewis at such a difficult time (right after the WEDDING FIASCO, as the police liked to call it) about a mere moonlight flit: 'They were paid in advance anyway so they weren't too bothered. Quite relieved, in fact, not to have to do the full cooked breakfast.'

'THEY did it!' Jen cried, suddenly convinced that people with a bad attitude to breakfast could well be murderers.

The police were getting pretty annoyed by now with Jen and her PATHETIC accusations. *Enough of zis talk*, they wanted a CONFESSION!

'Where were you the morning after the wedding, when the murders took place?' she was asked.

'On my HONEYMOON.'

'What honeymoon? You're not married!'

'A mere technicality. I went ALONE.'

'How do we know you weren't hiding in the glen, waiting to pounce on your brother and Urma Thurb?'

Jen wished they would stop calling it the 'glen'. It was a GORGE, a geological vulval cleft. The police make everything sound so PALTRY, seedy, and stale. So MALE.

'I was not waiting to pounce on anyone,' she said icily. 'I was trying to get AWAY from everybody. I needed to get away IMMEDIATELY!'

Then she told them all about her train ride and the Kindergarten Lady and the crumby hotel and the old dolls who dropped their PEAS and the hotel manager and the fish-and-chip shop people and her ACCOSTER and the nice guy with the high voice and the NAKED guy, and even about her night spent naked in the wilderness: this was turning into a veritable ALIBI.

The police were very dubious about the whole business, especially that night in the woods – just the kind of thing MURDERERS do – and the fact that she used an ALIAS at the hotel (LOATHE SELF!) didn't help. But her story checked out! It seemed that Jen was even more conspicuous than she'd always FELT: everybody who'd SEEN her remembered her! From the ticket collector who'd known on sight that Jen was a Standard-Class Super Saver, to the hotel manager and his serving-wench girlfriend (who'd been talking about Jen BEHIND HER BACK ever since her brief stay), and the fish-and-chip fryers who'd wondered why she needed so many CHIPS, and the Kindergarten Dope and the nice guy with the high voice.* Even people JEN didn't remember remembered HER. Boy, did they remember her: the biggest bride they'd ever seen, with BLOOD all over her dress!

* The police had by now taken the Shetland sweater-dryer and the candlesticks away for forensic tests (though killing people with candlesticks is so passé). Thus, for Jen, it was back to the DRAWING BOARD, vis-à-vis drying her cargo pants!

'That was TOMATO!' Jen said, but no one believed her. The nice guy with the high voice had already sent her wedding dress to the cleaner's, so all trace of the vindicating tomato stains was gone! (He'd even had the PETTICOATS repaired.)

'What about the NAKED guy?' Jen asked rather wistfully. 'Did *he* remember me?'

'We haven't talked to him.'

'Why not?!'

'He's in prison. Unreliable witness.'

'What's he in prison for? Being NAKED? That's not a real crime. Or IS it?'

'Breach of the peace and causing a commotion in a public thoroughfare –'

'Public thoroughfare? But *he's* a member of the public! Why shouldn't he make use of public thoroughfares? This is just what he SAID would happen: he's been locked up for having a BODY!'

This TONE of Jen's was doing her no favours. The police thought it bore every resemblance to the callous tone of a MURDERER (they HATED all her capital letters!). And she seemed to care more about a NAKED GUY than she did about her own BROTHER. Pretty suspicious. Also, she was SO FAT! Too fat to be allowed to roam free. Too fat to be BELIEVED.

BODY OF EVIDENCE

WHAT A MESS. Murder's messy! Everyone in that little rural backwater was affected by it, even Dr Lewis. He wasn't happy that his nurse and sometime FIANCÉE (and still current MAIN SQUEEZE) was being repeatedly questioned by police about the possibility that she'd cut two people up and hidden the pieces in HANDBAGS under BUSHES, not happy at all.

Many of his PATIENTS felt the same: a number of them, already perturbed by Jen's genitalia insights, signed a PETITION against Jen for being a back-stabbing backwater-invading handbag-hoarding doctor-nabbing MMR-jabbing meringuelike BUTTERBALL. They were all talking about her behind her back – when they weren't talking about FRANCINE, that is. Francine was the best bit of gossip they'd had in *years* (even better than a MURDER). Her loyal receptionist work, her secretive but enviable connection to Dr Lewis, the meek non-entity CHILDREN, her mother phobia, her plastic-surgery adventures, her many manic EPISODES, now retrospectively deduced, had inflamed imaginations for miles around!

All of these excitements were having an effect on Dr Lewis's general DEMEANOUR: he was becoming DISORGANISED. The usual stuff doctors do was becoming a BURDEN to him. He was starting to make *silly mistakes*. His usual systematic style was unravelling! NOW, when he gave people morphine injections disguised as flu jabs, he sometimes forgot to SAY it was a flu jab, which kind of wrecks the JOKE. Some patients asked QUESTIONS, some got away! He also gave penicillin to people who were allergic to it – but not with his previous pleasure.

For distraction, he carried on with redecorating the surgery, though so far he'd only repainted the ceiling in the consulting room, and moved a few piss-soaked chairs around. One of the chairs was now in the waiting room, where ALL the chairs were piss-soaked; the other was in Francine's station where it wasn't needed, since Francine had a high-tech SWIVEL chair of her own.

After the move, the chairs CREAKED a lot, as if they were trying to CONTACT each other, saying, 'Where'd YOU end up?' or just, 'How's tricks?' If only chairs COULD talk, a pretty tale they'd tell of the asses they have known! The police could have INTERVIEWED them. But the police didn't interview the chairs – they were only interested in JEN. They had now found the MURDER WEAPON, not the Shetland sweater-dryer after all but a knife from a knife SET given to Jen and Roger as a wedding present. The rest of the set was in Roger's quarters but, as he'd told the police, anyone could have taken one from there at any time.

Roger had found a way of cheering Jen up during this difficult period. No, ANOTHER way. He took her in his Jag to buy handbags! In her present state of confusion and bereftitude, Jen could only face buying one at a time (in better days, she could have bought ten or TWENTY, if she had the dough!), but Roger was patient. He could wait. He knew how hard it was to select a handbag, how much SOFTNESS was required, how many RIDGES, compartments, SPANGLES, and the choices to be made between different properties of leather, felt, cloth, straw and plastic, woven, quilted, or covered with TASSELS. It's COMPLI-

CATED. Roger was in the KNOW about handbags, and he could wait. That's what he kept telling Jen. Even if she had to go to PRISON, he would wait. FOR EVER!

They had just returned from one of these expeditions when three policemen jumped out at them from a bush. Jen WISHED they wouldn't DO that. She had just started to LIKE that particular bush, the first hydrangea she had ever properly LOOKED at, and now they were WRECKING it. Jen hadn't even got her new RETICULE as far as the VESTIBULE yet, and already they were accusing her of having murdered her brother and Urma Thurb! It was intolerable.

'WHY would I kill them?' she shrieked. She was about to go on, but she couldn't BREATHE. Jen was suffocating, ASPHYXIATING. She was turning NAVY-BLUE. In acute need of liberation, privacy, OXYGEN, she rushed inside and, with effort, climbed the stairs to the ROOF. She felt like she was coming up for air from the bottom of the SEA, like an aged coelacanth who'd decided to EVOLVE. Out on the widow's walk she could breathe again. And there, to the still air, the still birds, the still night, Jen sighed, 'Why would I kill them? I LOVED them!'

She didn't think she could be heard by the men below, but there was something about that stillness and the accoustical oddities of the building: Jen's widow's-walk words carried down to Roger and the policemen, and they were all REVOLTED to hear that Jen loved anybody. The police didn't even want her in their CAR now! NOBODY wants to be stuck for long inside a vehicle with someone so fat and so LOVING. The police wanted nothing more to do with Jen! To her amazement and relief, they zoomed off.

Filled with renewed hope of REPRIEVE, ESCAPE, VINDICATION (RESCUE?), Jen raced down the stairs to Roger's trim waist, swivelling hips, and cleft chin. He met her halfway. It was an AWKWARD moment, since there was no getting past each other on the narrow staircase, and

Roger seemed so ALOOF. Jen offered to make him STETHOSCOPE-shaped PASTA, but all Roger said was, 'You're fired.' Then he did somehow manage to squeeze past her, and stalked upstairs to his flat and his FAMILY.

It was the latest, and laziest, of betrayals. Jen lurched down to her lair to lick her wounds. The thought of Roger with his kids was EXCRUCIATING. Fuck kids.

Jen lay on her bed looking up at the few handbags that newly adorned her walls. But now the sight of them made her GAG. She couldn't imagine handbags any more that were not stuffed with the soft tissues of Nicky and Urma Thurb! How could ROGER bear to look at them? Why did he encourage her to BUY them? Jen turned grey, as grey as her body might have been if she were no longer IN it. For she had finally realised something: HE did it, ROGER killed them.

And it was true! While Jen was galavanting around eating huge breakfasts and consorting with NAKED GUYS, Roger had been cutting breasts and asses off her nearest and dearest and playing with their ORGANS. Some he ATE, some burned, some buried; some he dissolved in ACID. As a first venture into body disposal (and DISPERSAL), it wasn't bad. He took a certain pride in his work, and longed to share some of his anatomical findings with Dr Kildare! Murder is such a lonely business (even with THRASH ROCK).

NOT QUITE WHITE
(A FLASHBACK)

Urma Thurb awoke, the morning after the wedding, filled with the white rage of RIGHTEOUSNESS. She too had read *Jane Eyre*. EVERYBODY reads *Jane Eyre* (doesn't mean it's a good book!). Before leaving town, Urma Thurb intended to have a WORD with Dr Lewis. She knew how to DO it (she'd passed all her exams). Urma Thurb's reprimands were dreaded in paediatric departments across the land!

Dr Lewis was sitting in his consulting room, ready to be CONSULTED – as if nothing had happened! He'd been expecting Martha to turn up but she hadn't arrived. New boyfriend perhaps. But what good was THAT? Martha needed fifteen new boyfriends a DAY. Dr Lewis had tried everything: steroids, anti-depressants and morphine. Hydrotherapy had proved useless, ELECTROTHERAPY too (he'd considered COMBINING them and finishing her off for good!). And ever since he'd HIT her jokingly once with a bunch of her NOTES, Martha had had a bit of a crush on him. Martha's crushes were huge aching THROBBING things, SCARY really. He was just too good-looking. Had the time come, he now mused in his swivel chair, to cut the VASAL NERVE?

Mid-morning. Francine would soon be coming in with his ELEVENSES. He should have been on his HONEYMOON by now. They had planned to drive to KILLIN in the Jag –

Jen had vetoed more exotic destinations. A pity, since Roger was owed a free trip somewhere by several drug companies in return for hooking his patients on their products. It would be nice to relax in Belize after all this hullabaloo, or the *BUSH* perhaps. But these daydreams were interrupted by a quiet knock on the door.

'Come in, Francine!' he called out merrily (marriedly).

'It's not Francine,' growled Urma Thurb, stiffly shutting the door behind her.

He offered her a chair, but she wouldn't take it. He even offered her a go on his SWIVEL chair, ordered specially from a company in NORWAY that made chairs with lumbar-protecting properties. 'It's pneumatically complicated,' he assured her.

'You have broken that poor girl's heart,' Urma Thurb began. 'What were you thinking? You are not free to MARRY.'

'Norwegian. Best money can buy – what?'

'How dare you put a vulnerable young woman through such an ordeal? What for god's sake was the POINT?'

'That is a matter for me and my conscience,' Dr Lewis solemnly replied.

'CONSCIENCE! Don't give me that,' snapped Urma Thurb. 'We're both medical people!'

'OK. Let's just say it's PRIVATE, between Jen and me.'

'Not so private YESTERDAY, when you revealed yourself and your, I must say, appalling circumstances to everyone in the village!'

'It's HARD bringing up kids on your own,' whined Roger (a guy who had orphaned DOZENS with his Munchausen theories). 'I don't want to be alone.'

'It seems to me you're not alone ENOUGH, sir. I think Jen was wise to leave and I hope she has the sense never to return.'

'LEAVE? Where's she gone?' asked Roger, who hadn't had a chance to check on Jen's whereabouts yet that morning: he'd just assumed she was in her office.

'How do *I* know?' answered Urma Thurb. 'She's disappeared. I haven't seen her since the wedding. I was talking to a few of your PATIENTS though. A woman named Martha. Also Frieda, the one with the disfigured baby? And a sickly-looking girl named Janet – ring any bells? You gave her father sleeping pills to kill himself with. And then there was someone named Sylvie, a very nice young woman who seems to have doubts about the way her AUNT died during a routine appointment – she wasn't even ILL.'

'Why are you bothering me with all these worthless people now?'

'Why?! Because, from what I've been hearing, Dr Lewis, your practice is scandalous, and possibly ILLEGAL.'

Roger considered pressing the PANIC BUTTON, another intrinsic feature of his swivel chair (people panic a lot in NORWAY?). But that would have brought Francine (with or without TEA), and Francine would no doubt panic too! So instead he theatrically covered his face with his hands, allowing only his chin cleft to peek through. But Urma Thurb was UNMOVED by Dr Lewis's chin cleft! Instead, she was gazing loftily at the ceiling with a cold and critical eye.

'You've really fucked up!' she muttered.

'OK, *OK*.'

'No, I mean THERE, in the corner!'

'*WHAT*?' he quirked, looking up in alarm. Urma Thurb pointed out the corner of the cornice which, he now saw, sported a spot of yellowed paintwork – Dr Lewis must have forgotten about that bit when he fell off the ladder on to JEN, all those months back! It looked TERRIBLE. He was surprised he hadn't noticed it before. How he hated anything OFF-WHITE.

Urma Thurb, after many happy hours spent with her handyman hubby, was ADEPT at identifying an emulsion mistake. She was not to know this was the LAST such mistake she would ever identify, in fact the last remark she would ever make on interior decoration of any kind!

It was brave, but foolish, of Urma Thurb to impugn Dr Lewis's DIY skills. He was TOUCHY about such things. He was crushed, CRUSHED, by her ceiling comment – and Roger Lewis didn't like being crushed (except by JEN). He now sprang from his swivel chair (lumbar spine in FINE shape), and stuffed a handkerchief into Urma Thurb's mouth so that Francine would not be upset in any way, should Urma Thurb put up a struggle. He then bound the indignant Urma Thurb's hands and feet with surgical tape, and injected her with lignocaine, which induces fits, then heart failure.

Jen's flat being conveniently VACANT, he dragged the dying Urma Thurb down there and hid her under Jen's bed for the time being. Busy man. Couldn't keep patients waiting. He'd decide what to do with the body later. The BODY. The body is such a burden.

NEXT!
(ANOTHER FLASHBACK)

Dr Lewis was just going back upstairs when the door above opened and Nicky came racing down. They met halfway. Nicky did not seem *pleased* by this convergence – he seemed ANGRY.

'Where's Jen?' he asked gruffly.

'Gone,' said Roger. 'She's disappeared!'

Nicky alarmingly grabbed Roger by the throat! 'Understandable after the stunt you pulled, you bastard.'

Not another one! 'Hey, watch it,' choked Roger, still quirking as best he could.

But Nicky rudely affixed his thumbs to Roger's CLAVICULAR FOSSA – without even ASKING. Roger now remembered Nicky was a DENTIST: the guy probably had a pretty good idea how to manipulate the NECK. But was it his intention to TWIST or to STRANGLE? Roger was beginning to REGRET letting Jen invite a few of her own people to the wedding. But he hadn't noticed that Nicky had any FEELINGS for Jen (apart from boredom, shame and irritation). Strange time to be getting an ERECTION, but Roger had one anyway!

Unlike Urma Thurb's moral righteousness, Nicky's resolve was made shaky by GUILT: he had after all been planning to SEDUCE Roger at some point, brother-in-law or not. But that was before he'd seen the state of Roger's FLAT. The guy's home-life was a HORROR. He lived like an ape! And into this jungle he had attempted to inveigle Nicky's one remaining RELATION.

But now Nicky was torn: he had an enticing view of the old CHIN CLEFT, and, following the line down through Roger's clavicular fossa, past his STETHOSCOPE, to his ERECTION – Nicky decided to unseam him LATER.

Sensing a lull in hostilities, Dr Lewis urged Nicky to accompany him to Jen's bedroom, where they could talk more privately, undisturbed by duty. So down they went, through Jen's living room, past Jen's kitchen and Jen's bathroom, where sat Jen's jacuzzi, unused, and into Jen's BEDROOM where, despite every dissuasive JEN FACTOR so far listed, they carried on with their intention to screw, cavorting unthinkingly (as is usually best).

Afterwards, lying on the bed together, they gazed up at the many hundreds of handbags: it was like a bedouin TENT in there! Taking it all in, Nicky said, 'My whole family's insane.'

'Oh, I LIKE those handbags!' said Roger loyally.

'Did you KNOW our mother was completely off her rocker?'

'Just because she jumped from a train? Probably postpartum depression,' counselled Roger sagely.

'She did other stuff too,' said Nicky. 'This was a woman who threatened to kill herself if the gas man came to read the meter before she'd had a chance to dust inside its CUPBOARD. Easily embarrassed, my mother. And she HATED kids, BABIES especially, the way they SMELL. She used to swing Jen out of the window by her FEET to give her some AIR. She's had BREATHING trouble ever since!'

'Well, I'M not embarrassed about anything,' Roger remarked irrelevantly, before realising he WAS embarrassed about something . . . what was it? Oh yes, the presence of Urma Thurb under the bed!

Nicky squirmed out of Roger's arms and stood up to get a better look at the handbags. 'What the fuck is she doing with all these – hey, that's MINE!' Nicky reached up to unhook a red-and-white-checked fanny-pack. 'Where'd she get this? Must've STOLEN it. It doesn't suit her! She's got no TASTE, that girl. No fashion sense. Those cargo pants she wears!'

Nicky's absorption in the bag gave Roger the chance to study his ASS. But it wasn't HALF the ass Jen's was! Nicky's was undimpled, unAMPLE. No chance of ever being overwhelmed by such an ass, no chance of being SMOTHERED. Roger missed JEN! *Come back to me*, he called to her in his head, *come back*! 'Come back!' he said out loud, by accident.

'Just a sec.' Nicky was in the middle of unzipping his fondly remembered bag. 'What the fu –' he said as he caught sight of the old POTATO PEELINGS Jen had put in long ago to fester, along with various jottings of scorn and disillusionment. It had obviously been SLIMY in there for a while, but now it was merely ENCRUSTED, like the pouch of a dead marsupial. 'This is DISGUSTING!' cried Nicky.

Dr Lewis was unnerved. Had Nicky found some of Roger's EMISSIONS in there? (Roger couldn't remember any more WHICH handbags he'd had carnal knowledge of, there were so many!) To distract Nicky from the bags, Roger pulled him back down on the bed, kissing him and murmuring sweet Latinate medical terms, then launched into his favourite form of pillow-talk: a lecture on FORMICATION (the sensation of ants crawling under your skin). This he accompanied with a dazzling amount of tickling, to illustrate the subject.

Nicky had always been a sucker for doctors. MESMERISED by Roger's antics, he lay with his eyes shut and an arm dangling over the side of the bed. When he felt a hand in his, he squeezed it passionately. But there was no reaction. Playing the aloof doctor, eh? Nicky brought the hand to his mouth and BIT it playfully. STILL nothing! This wasn't ALOOFNESS, this was total INSENSIBILITY! Nicky opened his eyes and stared at the hand. It had RINGS on it, rings put there by Urma Thurb's HUSBAND. For this was

URMA THURB'S HAND, connected to Urma Thurb's BODY no doubt, which was lying, red and dead, under the bed!

Way down at the other end of the bed, tirelessly trying to simulate formication on Nicky's toes, Roger somehow knew the game was up. He could tell Nicky knew something, and Roger didn't feel comfortable knowing that he knew that Nicky knew that Roger knew that Nicky knew that Roger knew he KNEW something. Not comfortable at all. Dr Lewis's settled life was at stake, his lucrative medical practice, his kids, his standing in the community. HOT DRINKS. (Trips to Belize.) Dr Lewis had a SYSTEM, and he was sticking to it.

WORTHLESS

Fired and furious, Jen leapt from her bed and began to pace her den. Like a FOX, she sulked and skulked. She tried to believe Roger INNOCENT of the murders of her brother and Urma Thurb. When that proved impossible, she decided to seek JUSTICE. But the police would never believe her and her INTUITION, the intuitions of the prime suspect! They'd think she was just griping because she'd been *fired*.

Also, Roger was a DOCTOR. Nobody likes to think ill of a doctor! Even though HE thought all his patients were WORTHLESS, they thought *he* was worth a great deal. Roger's patients were willing to DIE to protect his right to kill them! They were like those people who went on defending their BUTCHER – even buying MEAT from him – after he'd already admitted fatally poisoning thirty customers with *e coli*!

The loyalty of Roger's patients gave Jen an idea. She had no evidence on the murders of Nicky and Urma Thurb, but upstairs were hundreds of dubious DEATH CERTIFICATES (Jen had filed them herself!) of trusting patients who'd died surprisingly soon after seeing Roger. Now, Jen was no PURIST. She had killed the odd BABY herself, but never on this SCALE, never so systematically. Roger had killed whole SWATHES of people. Without him this rural backwater might have been a TOWN by now!

Jen snuck back upstairs at five in the morning and stuffed a carrier bag full to BURSTING with the dubious death certificates. Then she lugged it over to the police station a couple of miles away. She was kept waiting for HOURS. She felt like she was already in JAIL: the hot drinks machine was LOUSY. By the time she was finally allowed in to see the inspector, she was having trouble BREATHING.

'I know who did it,' she gasped. 'At least, I have an INKLING.' They plonked her in a chair and, sitting as close as they could bear to, tried to hear what she had to say. But they refused to countenance any nasty insinuations against Dr Lewis. He was a GP! (Even the police need their authority figures.) So then she whacked them with the death certificates. But the police weren't interested in death certificates! (They TOO hated paperwork.)

So Jen hauled her sorry ass out of there while the going was still good – they said they'd be arresting her any day now, they were just waiting for a few more lab results (the police are like DOCTORS with their fucking LAB RESULTS). Exhausted from the torments of the night, and FREEZING in her summer cargo pants, Jen looked longingly at a taxi as it sped through a puddle, splashing her. But she couldn't afford a TAXI. She had no job! I HAVE NO JOB.

Unbeknownst to Jen, the taxi driver himself had doubts about Dr Lewis! He had often had to drive people to the surgery, people who never came out! Francine would walk over to the car and say, 'Don't bother waiting, so-and-so's dead. We've called the morgue.' It happened so often that the taxi driver had begun to DREAD taking anyone to Dr Lewis's surgery! He dreaded the turrets, the widow's walks, the strangely elongated chimney pots, and the hydrangeas. But he never TOLD anyone – he was scared of being sued.

A CITIZEN'S ARREST

Dr Lewis was on call as usual, the morning after he fired Jen. He had no idea she was out REPORTING HIM TO THE POLICE. He thought she was sleeping in, the LAZY COW, now that she was JOBLESS.

Roger felt oddly TRIUMPHANT for so adroitly extricating himself from Jen's clutches and distancing himself from the prime murder suspect at the same time! It made him look WHITER THAN WHITE, or so he HOPED. He had always WANTED to look whiter than white. He should have done it before. But he'd been swayed by that ASS. Yes, the swaying of that ass had almost been his RUIN. It interfered with his all-important WORK.

DAVID was his first patient of the day. He'd come to discuss getting treatment for Hepatitis C. David had only just discovered he *had* Hepatitis C. He had gone to give blood, as he did every year, and a few weeks later the blood bank called him up to say they didn't WANT his blood, they didn't want anything more to DO with him, because he had Hepatitis C (caught apparently from a blood transfusion as a child). David was still in shock.

Dr Lewis barely knew what Hepatitis C WAS, but told David sternly that he ought to have his WIFE tested as well. But, as David now explained, she HAD been tested, and she too had Hepatitis C! Dr Lewis countered this by advising

David to have his three CHILDREN tested. But they had already been tested, and THEY had Hepatitis C. This was getting silly! Dr Lewis might have been able to muster up some sympathy for one or TWO cases of Hepatitis C, but FIVE? Come ON.

Next was MIMI, who was having a nervous breakdown because her husband had run off with a younger woman. Forgetting that the only thing to do in such circumstances is to cut holes in his SUITS and give his WINE away, Mimi had succumbed instead to panic attacks, insomnia and weeping spells.

'But men are PROGRAMMED to lose interest in women your age, Mimi,' Roger explained. 'It's the *law*, I mean it's the law of natural selection. You see, in the early days of Man, anyone attracted to older women, past their childbearing days, would lose his chance to contribute genetically to the next generation. So that kind of guy DIED OUT. It's an evolutionary FACT.'

He thought he'd put it clearly enough but would have gone on (and ON), had his concentration not been disturbed by JEN'S noisy entrance. She stomped over to the desk and threw a big carrier bag full of papers on to it.

'I couldn't leave them alone with you for a MINUTE, could I, Roger?' Jen asked. 'How *could* you? How could you kill my brother?!'

Roger bustled the mystified Mimi out of the room.

'How would you like it if I killed YOUR brother?' Jen demanded.

'I don't HAVE a brother,' quirked Roger.

'What a line!' said Jen. 'That's the kind of thing that KILLED VAUDEVILLE!' Jen pointed to the carrier bag. 'Those are death certificates, the death certificates YOU falsified. All THREE HUNDRED of 'em. I'm taking them to the police!' (A bluff, since she'd just got BACK from the fucking police.)

Roger sat down again in his swivel chair and idly fingered the corners of some of the pages that were sticking out of the bag. Jen snatched them out of his reach. 'No funny business, Roger. I've made photocopies.' (Another bluff.)

'Why're you making such a FUSS?' he asked gently, genuinely perplexed.

'WHY? Because Nicky and Urma Thurb were all I had!' Jen cried. 'Besides YOU. And they were MEDICAL people, Roger. You don't kill COLLEAGUES.'

'They were in the way,' Roger offered. 'They came between us. And they got in the way of my WORK.'

'So you ADMIT it!' said Jen, momentarily stunned. Then she started to shake. She turned ORANGE with fury, a lifetime's fury. 'How DARE you? Now I'm going to have to make a Citizen's Arrest.'

But before she could figure out HOW you make a Citizen's Arrest, Roger jabbed her twice in the ass with a big syringe! Even though her ass was numb, Jen definitely felt two jabs. What was in it? Diamorphine? How MUCH? Was Jen going to DIE before she saw justice done??

Jen fought like a RHINOCEROS that had just been shot with a TRANQUILLISER dart: fiercely. She tore at Roger's yellow hair and white coat. She bit his stethoscope in two! She butted him repeatedly with her rhinoceros HEAD, and finally SAT on him with her rhinoceros BUTT. Roger GIGGLED at first but quietened as he searched Jen's ass more and more desperately for AIR POCKETS. Then he conked out!

TENACIOUS OF LIFE

Roger woke a few hours later to find himself inside the Air Ambulance helicopter! Comforting to see old Charlie at the helm. But where were they going? It seemed a bit dark for one of their missions (Roger preferred morning flights). But always there is DUTY.

He started to get up, but couldn't move! He was tied down! What was going on? Then he heard Jen.

'Don't try anything, Roger,' she said.

She is TENACIOUS OF LIFE, thought Roger: he'd given her enough morphine to kill an ELEPHANT! (But not a rhinoceros.)

'You're tenacious of life!' he quirked, looking about for her in the dark.

Jen turned away in disgust and yelled to Charlie over the hellish din, 'Our patient seems to have revived.'

Charlie twisted round in his (NON-swivel) seat, smiling, and said, 'Hey, mate. We were worried about you!'

'*I* wasn't,' said Jen. 'By the way, Charlie, there's been a change of plan. We're not going to the hospital. That was a LIE.'

'WHAT?!' Charlie could barely *hear* Jen, but he didn't like her TONE. (Jen's tone never did her any favours.)

Jen held up a syringe and tested it for air bubbles. 'One false move and I'll let you both have it!' she warned. (Isn't it great how watching a lot of dull movies prepares you for this kind of occasion? The hoodlum parlance just seemed to come naturally.) 'This is BOTULIN SERUM,' she told them (another bluff). 'The BAD news is that a long and painful death awaits you if you cross me. There's no known antidote – but I don't have to tell YOU GUYS that! The GOOD news is you'll die without a wrinkle on you!'

Roger tried to wrench himself free of his bonds with the use of his strong biceps, triceps, abductor pollicis longus and brachialis muscles, along with his gastrocnemius, his subscapularis, his brachioradialis, his trapezius, his pronator quadratus, infraspinatus, rectus abdominus, tensor fasciae latae, adductor magnus muscles, and his deltoids. He tried EVERYTHING! But it didn't work! Jen repositioned him on his stretcher without much difficulty.

'A little cramped in here, isn't it?' she said. 'Not that you minded that the FIRST time we met!'

'What the hell are you talking about?'

'The first TIME, our first SCREW. Don't tell me you've forgotten! In the loo on the PLANE, Roger!'

The adrenalin produced by his present predicament must have acted as an *aide-memoire*, for at last Roger did have a dim recollection of their first encounter! He remembered that ASS at least.

Aeroplanes are the source of all human misery.

Jen now told Charlie to fly to a well-known local landmark, an isolated thrashing COCK of ROCK that lay a quarter-mile offshore.

'But why?' asked Charlie in dismay. 'In THIS weather?' A GALE was blowing.

'Don't listen to her, Charlie,' yelled Roger. 'She's NUTS.'

'You sure know a lot of crazy women, Roger,' said Jen. 'Did it ever occur to you that YOU might be the common denominator? Maybe you drive us all crazy.'

'Red Alert, Charlie! Code N,' yelled Roger. 'Six o'clock. About face! STOP!'

But Charlie turned out to be quite in AWE of botulism. He accordingly changed course and flew judderingly towards the sea. Snow beat against the windscreen as they lost the last of the light.

There was no hope of landing in such a storm when they reached the rock. The helicopter was jouncing all over the place! Its jerks and jumps were making it hard for Jen to balance the syringe on her knees while she sorted out the ropes of the lowering gear, but she managed somehow. She cautiously released Roger's limbs, one at a time, just long enough to attach him to his HARNESS. He begged her to reconsider. 'What about my KIDS? My patients? FRANCINE? They need me!'

But *Jen* had also needed him. Opening the hatch below (NOT a euphemism for Jen's SNATCH), she dislodged him from his comfy stretcher and sent him whirling and twirling into the night, as she slowly unwound the rope. For Jen was at the end of her tether too.

'There you go, Roger,' she yelled when he finally landed on the rock. 'Your free trip!'

JUST JELLY

Roger is all alone in the dark on the brink of time. He feels like the last person on earth! No east or west, no HORIZON. No one to help him. All around him only darkness and water. How far to shore? A MILE? Half a mile perhaps. He'll die of exposure trying to swim. Wouldn't last FIVE MINUTES in that sea.

The helicopter has COPPED OUT on him. Little chance of its returning before he PEGS OUT. As an embryo, Roger Lewis was all HYALINE CARTILAGE. Now he's just JELLY.

Standing in his white coat atop the icy wastes, he stares in disbelief at the gannets and guano. Roger has always been troubled by anything OFF-WHITE, and he's troubled by it now.

How DARE she do this to me? After I commingled so willingly in the basement, and my JAG. Even on a PLANE, it seems! Cunt. Why do women have to be such a PAIN IN THE ASS?

He stumbles along the slippery surface of the ancient imperturbable rock, seeking shelter from the wind and snow. He's forgotten about the LIGHTHOUSE, if he ever knew of its existence, and fails to see it in his confusion. He sees only CLIFFS, cliffs of fall frightful.

Every solution seems hopeless. He grips an icy boulder to

look over the edge, and can just make out an almost perpendicular SLIDE along one corner of the rock, leading to the dark waves below. The white sea foam forms C-shapes amongst the stones. All Roger can SEE now are these C-shapes.

It's too steep and slippery to CLIMB down, and there's no way of getting back UP. Even if he manages not to fall OFF the slide on the way down, he will probably gather so much speed he'll crack his head on the rocks at the bottom and hit the water UNCONSCIOUS, never even getting a CHANCE to swim.

Roger stands up, bracing himself against the wind that seems to come from all directions at once. He's already numb with cold. He has never been so alone, so angry, so afraid, or so doomed to die. He peers across the water at the shadowy land, near land, DEAR land! His urge to rejoin his species is ACUTE.

He looks again at the icy promontory with its perilous slide. It's worth a try.

LIFE!

As soon as he escaped from Jen's clutches and her fake BOTULIN SERUM, Charlie flew swiftly back to the rock to search for Roger. But he couldn't find him! Roger's BODY was discovered by some fishermen weeks later, bloated and offensive. It had been nibbled by coelacanths, but was still recognisable: the chin cleft was intact.

Jen was tried for helicopter-hijacking, GP-kidnapping, paramedic-frightening, bag-snatching, peace-breaching, and triple homicide. JEN was bloated and offensive too and was sentenced *on these grounds alone* to Life Imprisonment – the Home Secretary said she'd NEVER get out!

But for Jen it was a kind of LIBERATION: she was free to hate herself in peace. She celebrated by refusing to wear clothes! The prison authorities, fearing Jen's misshapen form might incite other inmates to unrest, DISGUST, or an insurrection of like-minded behaviour, kept her in solitary confinement. She LOVED it! She became ALL BODY, one big land mass of off-white FLAB, her flesh dimpled and trembly, her skin covered with suppurating sores that erupted in an unending and unedifying cycle of quiescence and decay. She was despised and demonised to the end of her days, and had to have EXTRA HEAT in her cell.

But enough of zis talk. Take off your clothes!

A NOTE ON THE TYPE

The text of this book is set in Bembo. This type was first used in 1495 by the Venetian printer Aldus Manutius for Cardinal Bembo's *De Aetna*, and was cut for Manutius by Francesco Griffo. It was one of the types used by Claude Garamond (1480–1561) as a model for his Romain de L'Université, and so it was the forerunner of what became standard European type for the following two centuries. Its modern form follows the original types and was designed for Monotype in 1929.